Some Sort of Twilight

Carolyn Lewis

Watermark
Press

The Collection – first published in The New Welsh Review – 2001 – and reprinted with their kind permission.

Some Sort of Twilight – first published by Honno in the anthology My Cheating Heart in 2005 and reprinted here with their kind permission.

The Photographs – first published by Honno in the anthology Strange Days Indeed in 2007 and reprinted here with their kind permission.

Trolley Boss – first published by Route Magazine in the anthology Wonderwall in 2010 and reprinted here with their kind permission.

Living Over the Shop – first published by QWF in the anthology Dust of Time in 2011 and reprinted here with their kind permission.

For my daughters, Kathryn, Jo and Beth
and, as always, for Brian.

Published in UK by Watermark Press 2022

© Carolyn Lewis 2022

The moral right of Carolyn Lewis to be identified as the author of
this work has been asserted by her in accordance with the Copyright,
Designs and Patents Act, 1988

A CIP catalogue record for this book is available from the British Library

ISBN: 978 1 8380043 2 3

Typeset in Book Antigua

Cover design by nb-design.com

Printed by Imprint Digital

Watermark Press
Unit 77 Penn Street, Duo Tower, London, England, N1 5FF
www.watermarkpress.co.uk

Contents

A Bit of a Do

It was my thing, meeting Dave once a week. It gave me a sense of being able to offload, in the knowledge that he'd listen to me. How do kids say it? "*Thank you for sharing.*" I didn't say that to Dave, as he'd think I was mad. We were sort of related, though not really.

His daughter had married my son, and we met for the first time at a restaurant when Dave's daughter, Molly, got engaged to my son, Tom. We're roughly the same age; Dave is 56 and I'm 57, and we're similar in a lot of ways; we're both quiet, both interested in cars and both of us have dreamt about buying and restoring a Mini Cooper S. I suppose that's a bit sad. When those cars first came out, neither of us could afford one, and now they're almost *vintage*, we still can't afford one.

Dave and I can still dream though, and we do that once a week. Neither of us would ever *say* that we were dreaming, as that would be too embarrassing. We talk about gearboxes, about peak torque and whether the cars would need roll bars. We are lost in a world which we can inhabit for a couple of hours. We meet in the pub, the one at the edge of the park. It was strange that we'd both been drinking there for some time before we met each other properly. My wife, Sally, would say that it was a bloke thing. "So you *knew* each other then?", she said that at the restaurant when Dave and I shook hands. Although we'd give each other a nod across the bar, I would bet that if Dave and I had met outside the pub, we'd have had difficulty knowing where we'd seen

1

each other.

Anyway, it was a relief to be able to talk to Dave in the restaurant. Molly is a nice enough girl and I knew that my lad was besotted with her, even though Dave's wife, Lizzie, is (I'm not sure how to put this) a bit *fancy* for my taste. She wears lots of perfume, has perfectly manicured nails and, well to be honest, far too much cleavage on show, if you ask me. She's *loud*; I'd never really thought about that before, but her volume was too high. Sally liked her though. They got on like a house on fire, and before long, the six of us were paired off: Sally and Lizzie were laughing, Tom and Molly were clutching each other as if they were drowning, so Dave and I were left to talk.

It was the same throughout the whole wedding thing. That was quite a business, let me tell you. Sally kept going on about the outfits, what the wedding dress had cost, what Lizzie was wearing, there were hours and hours on the shoes, the flowers and the bridesmaids. It was the only conversation in our house for months. I couldn't think straight and, when I saw Dave in the pub and realised that he felt the same, well, it was as if I'd found a life raft.

Some sort of madness descended at the time of the wedding. I once told Sally that, even if a war had been announced, she wouldn't have paid any attention. "Oh, don't be daft, it's just that there's a lot to think about, and to do."

See, the thing is, I didn't understand that. It was Dave's daughter who was getting married. We were just the groom's parents, so not really in the thick of it at all.

Sally said I didn't understand. I don't suppose I did. I didn't then and I don't now.

We only have the one son, we lost a baby and they told us it was a girl and after that, well, there were no more. Molly is one of three daughters, and Dave often says that they'll bankrupt him,

2

but he never says it as if he means it.

Sally said we should offer to pay something towards the wedding. "You should talk it over with Dave," she told me. "It's the right thing to do."

Was it? I didn't know, I'm just an ordinary bloke and these things don't occur to me, but Sally went on and on about it. "They'll think we're mean if you don't," she added.

There never seemed to be the right opportunity to mention it. Dave and I had a few beers, we both walked to the pub and we talked about the Government (what a bunch of liars), we talked about our gardens, or at least I did; Dave didn't know an onion from a dandelion and, of course, we talked about cars. It was our thing. It sounds silly now when I think about it, but we said that if either of us won the lottery, we'd buy an old Cooper S or, to hell with it, we'd have one each. We'd want to work on them, to tune them until they were at their peak.

We both talked about it, we always laughed when we said it, but we both knew that if we had the money, we'd buy those cars. We rubbished the new Coopers, said they weren't a patch on the originals. What did we know? I drive a Ford and Dave has a Honda.

Anyway, as I said, I always looked forward to those hours with Dave in the pub.

As the day of the wedding grew closer, Sally was on another diet, moaning about her *bingo wings*. She was always narky with me, telling me that she couldn't sleep because of the worry. I asked our lad, Tom, how he was feeling. He grinned at me, "I'm all right, Dad. Just wish it was all over; you know what I mean." I did.

They were buying a house, him and Molly, just a few streets away. It was a bit of a wreck, but they were going to do it up. He's handy, my son, takes after me in that sense. He's an electrician and he talks about having his own business one day. Molly was a

3

primary school teacher, a clever girl, and I knew that Tom was proud of her career.

When the wedding day arrived, it felt almost like a relief. Sally had been awake half the night, tossing and turning, and nudging me to ask if I thought her fascinator was all right. How would I know what a *fascinator* was? I'd offered to pay for the wedding cars. Dave had thanked me, "Nice one, mate." Sally was right, I was glad I'd done that. They weren't Coopers though; they weren't big enough apparently.

Anyway, it went OK. Molly looked beautiful and I saw tears in my son's eyes when they were finally married; I almost shed a few myself. Lizzie had so much makeup on that her tears caused black streaks down her face from all the mascara. It looked a mess if you ask me.

It's funny how a day that had been planned, prepared and looked forward to for months, was over in a flash. It felt that no time had passed between leaving our house to go to the church, and before we knew it, we were in a taxi going home. I said that to Sally and she nodded, quietly saying, "I know. I feel as if I should have taken more notice."

I wasn't sure what she meant and I said something about seeing the photographs, and all the phones that were being held up, but she shook her head and said, "No, I didn't mean that."

There was a sort of ongoing *inquest* between Sally and Lizzie; they talked about various people: who'd had too much to drink, the argument between one couple, the peculiar shade of green one woman wore, and then Molly and Tom came back from their honeymoon and life settled down once again.

Dave and I met up, and we talked about plans for the cars, about whether Dave should buy a new shed and he said that he'd been around to see Molly and Tom's house and had painted a

4

bedroom for them. I said that I'd dug a part of their garden, and it seemed to me that our family had been extended and it felt good, although thinking about it now, we never met up again; that is, Dave and Lizzie and Sally and me, you know, to go out.

Sally mentioned it first, when she said it was odd that there didn't seem to be any mention of a bit of a do to celebrate Molly and Tom's first wedding anniversary. I looked at her, "Oh, come on, why would there be? Perhaps they just want to celebrate on their own. After all, it's only been a year."

Sally shook her head, "No, something's not right."

In the pub, Dave said that Lizzie had been to see Molly one afternoon during half-term and he said that his wife thought Molly was quiet. Dave shrugged, "I told her, the girl's probably tired; she puts in a long day."

I nodded my agreement and we talked about rugby, neither of us were football fans.

It was about a week later, and when I got home from work, Sally was in the kitchen and, even before I could take my jacket off she said, "Tom and Molly have separated."

"*What?* Don't be daft, they've only been married a year. What are you talking about?"

Sally shoved her hands in her pockets, and I could see she'd been crying. "Molly told our Tom that she'd made a mistake, and she wants a divorce."

"No, you've got that wrong. They've had a row, it's something and nothing." The strange thing was, I couldn't find the words I wanted to use. It had only been a *year*! The marriage won't have had a chance to get going, to work its way around the bumps along the way.

Sally glared at me. "I'm telling you. Tom's been here and he's in a right state; he says Molly won't see sense, she's moved back in with Dave and Lizzie, and she's talking to a solicitor. Oh God, it's such a mess."

"I'll talk to him." I said that without knowing what I'd say. "I'll ask him for a pint, just to see what's going on."

"It's not *Tom* you should be talking to; it's Molly. She's the one who's calling time on their marriage."

"Have you spoken to Lizzie? Does she know what it's all about?"

Sally shrugged, "Can't get much out of her, she said that Molly had gone all quiet; apparently she says she just doesn't want to be married any longer."

"Oh, for God's sake. They're kids, they don't know what they want. You and I had rows in the first year, didn't we? It's about finding out *how* to live with each other."

Sally ran her hands through her hair, "I don't know. I'm all over the place."

I put my arm around her, "Don't worry; it'll sort itself out. These things always do."

As it turned out, I saw Dave before I saw Tom. We met as we always did on a Wednesday evening and Dave had already got the pints in. He pushed one glass towards me, "Here, I reckon you'll need it."

I swallowed a mouthful of beer before speaking, "So, do you have any idea what's going on? Sally is walking around as if the world has come to an end." I kept my voice light, not wanting to give this *situation* any importance. It wasn't important; it couldn't be.

Dave looked at me, "All I know is that Molly says she's made a mistake and she wants a divorce. She says she's changed her mind about marriage."

I tried to laugh, wanting to say something to make Dave laugh, something like, "*Haven't we all felt like that?*" I didn't though, as he just didn't seem to be in the mood.

Dave shook his head, "She spends a lot of time in her room, her old bedroom that is, and sometimes I can hear her walking around downstairs at night, making herself cups of tea."

"...and what does Lizzie say? Has she spoken to Molly?"

Dave pulled a face, "Ah, that's a bit awkward."

"What is?"

Dave picked up his glass and stared at it. He cleared his throat, "Lizzie feels that this is all Tom's fault..."

"*Tom!* What's he done? Why does Lizzie...?" I didn't understand any of this.

Dave sighed, "Nothing to do with me, mate, this is just what Lizzie..." He stopped and looked at me, "Lizzie thinks that our Molly was a bit *overwhelmed* by your Tom." Looking away, his eyes fixed once more on the pint in front of him.

"I don't... What the... "What does that mean? *Overwhelmed!?*"

Dave shifted, "Lizzie thinks that your son might have bullied Molly into getting married."

He spoke softly and I didn't understand what he meant. I looked at him and then I leant forward, "Are you saying that my son is a bully? Is that it?"

Dave put a hand up, "No, *no!* That's not what I'm saying." He glanced around and his voice dropped, "It's just that Lizzie thinks our Molly might have been a bit young, or a bit, well you know, she hasn't fully grown up yet."

I sat back, winded. "My son is a gentle soul and he'd never, *ever* bully Molly. He just hasn't got it in him." I felt a build-up of anger and I wasn't sure where the anger should go. It wouldn't be to Dave; the poor sod was as uncomfortable as I was. Should it be at Lizzie? Well, maybe it could be, or perhaps it was Molly, trying to find a reason to end a marriage and thinking Tom was the obvious candidate. I wasn't having it. I bloody well wasn't.

Dave pulled a face, "Have you seen Tom? Have you had a chance to talk to him?"

"No, I haven't. To tell you the truth, Sally only told me yesterday and I promised I'd go and talk to Tom, to hear his side of the story."

"Well, when you do, let me know."

I nodded my agreement, and recognising that we both wanted to change the subject, Dave told me about a Cooper S he'd seen on his way to work. I felt the tension ease and drained my pint. "Want another one?"

I walked to the bar with our empty glasses in my hands. Weddings and nerves and upsets was a world I knew little about, but it seemed to be the norm. I *did* know that I'd talk to Tom as soon as I could. Sally had spoken to him and said she thought it would be a good thing for me to talk to him on my own. "It breaks my heart to see him," she said. Maybe she thought I wouldn't get so upset.

I went to see him and it broke *my* heart to see our son on his knees painting the skirting boards of the house that he and Molly had bought. I'd taken a few cans with me and Tom stopped painting as we sat in his kitchen. He'd not started on that yet and it was full of MDF units, flaky paint and damaged vinyl flooring. I remembered seeing Molly's face, and the way she'd frowned when she told me about how they were going to sand the floors downstairs and how she wanted terracotta tiles in the kitchen.

It was obvious that it was just Tom living in the house; the sink was full of mugs and plates, and pizza boxes were piled up by the back door. I nodded towards them, "Don't let your mother see those. You know how she'll go on about having a proper diet."

Tom shrugged, "Dad, it's all I can face right now."

He's my son; I've watched the changes in his face as he's grown

8

older and I could see changes in him now. Shadows like bruises were under his eyes, and his skin was waxy with tiredness. His hair needed cutting and he looked as if even the thought of having a shower was beyond him. I knew I couldn't tell his mother that part.

We sat and clinked the cans together, "*Cheers.*" Although it seemed a stupid thing to do and say, it did seem to help somehow.

"Do you want to talk about it?" I kept my voice low and soft, as if I was coaxing a nervous kitten out from under a chair.

He shrugged, "There's not much to say. Molly says she doesn't want to be married any longer. She says she's not ready for it."

I touched his arm, "… and what do you say?"

I saw tears in his eyes and I remembered seeing him cry on his wedding day. "You don't have to tell me anything if you don't want to."

When he sighed, the breath rushed from him, and it sounded as if it had been kept there for a long time. "I don't know, Dad. She'd been *off* for a while. I kept asking what the problem was and all she could say was that she was tired, too much marking to do, or that there were too many things she had to cope with."

"Maybe that's it, she's just tired, or overworked. Maybe if she took time off, I don't know, a couple of weeks or something…" I stopped because Tom was shaking his head.

"Dad, look, I've tried everything: a holiday, meals out, *days* out. God, I even suggested that we should have a cleaner even though we haven't got the money for that." He looked around the kitchen as if seeing it for the first time, "I ran out of things to suggest and then she left."

"Son, this isn't the end of the world. Let her have some space, time with her Mum and Dad. I know Dave; he's a good bloke. He'll talk some sense into her. She'll be back, I'm sure of it."

I was just using words, trying them out for size because I didn't know what else to do or say. Tom looked as if he'd been ambushed and I knew that he was as confused by the whole situation as I was. It made no sense. All sorts of thoughts were moving around in my head, things I wanted to ask but wouldn't. *Was it bedroom stuff?* I couldn't ask my son that; I just couldn't. He's a grown up, and anyway, it wasn't any of my business.

Tom sat up and looked around the kitchen and pulled a face. "D'you know, Dad, I get back from work and I work on the house all the time. Part of me feels that, if I get it finished, then maybe Molly will want to come back." He looked at me, "…and then the other part of me thinks that if she doesn't come back, then at least I'll have a house that I can put on the market."

"Oh, Tom, son." I shook my head; I didn't know what to say. I pushed the other can towards him. He nodded.

When I told Sally that it didn't look good, she glared at me. "What does that mean? What did you say? How did you leave it with Tom?"

"He's all over the place, he's still trying to get the house up together, but…" I shrugged, "it was difficult to know what to say or do."

"Oh for God's sake. You should have told him to go and see her, try and sort things out."

I looked at the anger on my wife's face although I knew that she was struggling with it too. "A year? How the hell can it all go wrong in one year?"

As it turned out, it went down the pan. Tom *did* go to see Molly, and he told me how painful it was, meeting her at her parents' house. "It was what she wanted, Dad but the whole time I knew Dave and Lizzie were in the kitchen, and I knew that they were *guarding* Molly." He looked at me then, "I'd never hurt her, never in a million years."

The funny thing about your kids is that they're always your kids and I wanted to put my arms around my son and tell him that I'd sort it, how I'd make it right. This was something I couldn't put right though. It felt to me as if Molly was on a mission and the divorce went through, dragging Tom along with it.

Sally was beside herself; she blamed Molly, and she swore blind that she'd never speak to Lizzie again.

She'd had a long conversation with Lizzie, and Lizzie came right out with it, saying, "All this is Tom's fault. He badgered her, kept going on about getting married. She felt steamrollered into it."

D'you know, I can't remember ever seeing Sally that angry before? She was all for going around to see Lizzie, apparently "to have it out with her".

I told her that it wouldn't do any good. "Best to leave it, love. We need to focus on Tom now, to get him through this."

That's exactly what we did. Their house was sold; they actually got a bit more than they paid for it too, because of all the work Tom had done. Our Tom bought himself a flat and somehow things settled down. He was still talking of having his own business and it was good to hear him talking like that again.

Sally wouldn't have any mention of Lizzie though, or Molly for that matter, and her face changed if you did. She still looks away even if I just say Molly's name in passing.

For me, the biggest loss of all, were my visits to the pub to meet Dave. We met a few times when the divorce was going through and, although it was good to see him, the whole thing...well, it felt like a mist swirling around us. We asked each other how things were, but I know that we were both relieved when we nodded and said, "All good, thank you."

It all happened one Wednesday, when Dave arrived a bit late and I could see straight away that he was bothered and agitated.

After I offered to get him a pint, he just shook his head, "No, mate, thank you, but I'm not stopping." He looked around the pub, not sure what he was looking for and then he said, "It's best if we don't meet again. I'm sorry but, well the truth is, Lizzie's on my case and…" he shrugged, "Sorry, mate, but I won't be coming here again."

"Oh," that flummoxed me but, truth was, I wasn't surprised. I knew Lizzie wasn't the sort of woman to be reasonable.

We shook hands and it was formal and sad. I've not been back to the pub since. I couldn't face it.

The weird thing is that I saw a Cooper S the other day, one of the original models; it was red with a white roof, just like the car we'd always talked about. I'd been to see Tom, to give him a hand with putting in a new sink. The Cooper S came up alongside my car at traffic lights.

The driver looked at me and something made me wave. It wasn't Dave in the car. How could it be? I felt pleased to have seen the car, I just wished I could tell Dave.

As Light as Air

There'd been no warning, nothing out of the ordinary. I'd eaten my supper, a Chinese takeaway with an extra portion of fried rice. I'd watched an episode of *Friends* and then I went to bed. I read for a while and I must have dozed off. When I opened my eyes, the duvet was draped over me, the book was on the floor. I was floating. There's no other word for it, I was floating three feet above my bed.

I couldn't make a sound, not even a small shriek, but my heart was thumping. I closed my eyes. This was a dream, what else could it be? I opened my eyes. Nothing had changed. I was still three feet above my bed. I put my hands out in front of me, the movement made my body rock. "Oh, God," my voice came out as a whisper. I took a deep breath and then, without warning, I rose higher. The duvet slipped to the floor as I gravitated towards the ceiling.

I saw a cobweb draped over the lampshade. I reached out to move it, but at that moment my head nudged against the ceiling. "Oooh," I whimpered. My fear had gone. I looked down, I saw a silver, hooped earring lodged behind my dressing table. I'd been looking for that for ages. I floated towards the window. Outside, a moth hurled itself against the glass.

I tried other positions. I lifted my right arm. I moved towards the right. I did the same with the left arm, I moved left. I laughed. I put my arms out in front and felt my body move forward. I was

Superwoman. I touched the lampshade, I gently knocked the cobweb, watching as it floated down towards the carpet.

Head first, I moved from the bedroom to the living room. I touched the black and white prints on the wall. I wondered about rearranging the furniture. Maybe the yellow chair would look better closer to the window. I hovered, simply looking at my home. My new-found skill, the fact that I could levitate, I didn't know what to do with it, or even what I *could* do with it.

The next day, when I awoke, I stared at the ceiling. It was a bland expanse of white, the only sign that I hadn't been dreaming was the lampshade which hung crookedly.

See, the thing is, I didn't know what to *do* with the fact that I could float. Who could I tell? Who'd believe me? I'm a big girl, I wear size 22 clothes. Mum always told me that I had big bones. I want to believe that. I like the thought that both my skin and muscles work harder, be bigger, just to support my bones.

My name is Cassie and I work in Human Resources for an insurance company. No one from my office has been to my home. No one has seen the canary yellow chair I bought in a sale. No one has sat on my IKEA sofa. No one has seen the black and white prints on my walls, prints of Paris, of Rome, of Madrid. No one has seen the framed photo of a group of smiling, wine-flushed faces from last year's Christmas party. In the photo, there is Fran, Mandy, Sarah, Ian, Dan and me.

Each morning, as I get dressed, I look at that photo. I look at the faces and I look at Dan standing next to me. When the photographer yelled "smile", I'd slipped my arm through Dan's. It was there, captured, I was holding on to Dan.

Dan is 38. He's married with twin daughters. His wife is Nina and his daughters are Hannah and Sophie. I've seen pictures of his family. Dan has photographs on his desk and on the windowsill behind him. Nina, she's achingly slender with a mass of curly, red hair. I know where Dan went to university, I know what his salary is and I know where he lives.

I always get into work before anyone else. It's important to me that I'm at my desk by 8.30, that my computer is switched on, that I'm seen to be working. I watch them file past my desk, I see their faces. They smile and say "Hello". Sometimes they mutter, "Sorry, the bus was late." I'm not in charge of time-keeping, but they say it anyway.

That morning, the one after I'd levitated, I decided to walk to work. I needed to think about what had happened, what it meant and whether it might happen again. My head was down, I watched the buckles on my black, suede loafers. I saw how they shivered each time I put my foot on the pavement. I heard the tinkling sound they made.

I thought about last night. It wasn't anything I could talk about, not even in a "You'll never guess what happened to me last night," sort of way. I didn't have that type of relationship with anyone in the office. I did think about telling Dan. I thought of the way his eyes would widen. I'd hear the unspoken thought about how anyone my size could possibly float. I couldn't tell him.

When I got to the office, it was almost 9 o'clock. I was out of breath. I walked to my desk. I heard a muted chorus of "Morning, Cassie." I felt their surprise. I was always in before everyone else. I sat at my desk and I switched on my computer.

At lunchtime, needing a break, I walked to the minimarket at the end of the street and bought a packet of tuna and sweetcorn sandwiches, and took it back to the office.

Dan was standing near the water cooler. "Hi, Cassie." He wore a blue shirt and I could smell his aftershave. It was lemony, light. I could also smell fabric conditioner.

He smiled, "We're thinking of taking the girls to France this summer."

"I love France," I told him. "Always wanted to go to Provence, to see the lavender fields."

Dan shook his head and laughed, "Ah, the girls wouldn't be interested in fields of lavender. No, it'll be a beach holiday for us."

That's the thing with Dan. He always talks about his family, about how clever the girls are, how hard Nina works. She's a solicitor.

I wanted to say something to him, to keep him there, to make him laugh. I saw the look on his face, a look that told me he couldn't think of anything else to say either. He nodded and went back to his desk.

Sarah was nearby, she works in sales and I've seen the way she looks at Dan. I've seen how she twists a section of her hair around her finger when he talks to her. I've heard her laugh when he tells a joke. I want to tell her to keep away from him. I know she doesn't think I'm a threat. I know she looks at me and all she sees is my bulk, nothing else. She thinks that she alone should talk to Dan, to hear his jokes. She thinks that, because she's slim and attractive, she has more *right* than I do. But she can't fly.

The day was like every other day and, the whole time I was in the office, I watched Dan. I watched the way he smiled, I heard his laugh, I listened to his phone calls, heard the polite way he spoke to customers. I'd told no one that I'd levitated, that I'd moved, light as a feather around my flat. I kept that to myself. I didn't want to see the look of incredulity, the look that said, "*You?* Floating? Yeah, right."

When I left the office, I caught the bus to my parents' house. I eat there once a week. My Mum thinks that I don't eat properly, she says I should keep my strength up. She cooks large meals,

meals from my childhood: cottage pies, beef stew with dumplings. She watches every mouthful I eat. She asks if it's all right, or if I would like another helping. Sometimes it's easier to say 'yes,' than to listen to the hurt in her voice when she asks what's wrong with it.

We ate beef, large slices of it, all over-cooked and swimming in gravy. The roast potatoes were huge, but they were edible. As Dad chewed his beef, I heard the clicking of his jaw. Dad retired a few years ago and now he spends his time just filling his time.

I don't know if my parents are happy. That's not anything we ever ask each other.

Dad doesn't understand what I do, neither does Mum. They limit their questions to "How's the job going?"

I say that it's fine and then it's never discussed again until the same question is asked the next week.

We sat there, I asked about the garden, whether Dad was planting runner beans again, what had been on TV and then I ate what Mum put in front of me. I kept my secret safe. Telling my parents that I could float would be the same as if I'd announced my intention to climb the Himalayas. It was something so far away from the world they lived in, they would never comprehend it. So, again, I kept quiet.

Mum doesn't understand why I live on my own. She still talks about 'your bedroom', she says that Dad was thinking of redecorating it. She asked what colour I'd like on the walls, or whether she should buy a new duvet for 'my' bed. She asks me why I pay rent for a small flat when there's a perfectly good room waiting for me at home. She adds that it's not as if I've got a boyfriend.

I shook my head, she says it all the time. I don't know why I said what I did, but I said it anyway, "Well, for your information, there is someone, someone at work."

She nudged Dad, "Hear that, did you hear what Cassie said?"

Dad nodded, he looked at me. He didn't say a word, but I could tell he knew I was lying.

I sat up straight, "His name is Dan and, well, it's early days."

Mum insisted on giving me food to take home. She put half a roast chicken, two slices of sponge cake, a box of shortbread biscuits into a carrier bag. "For your friend," she said. The coyness in her voice made my teeth ache, but I took the bag.

I caught the bus home, the weight of the meal I'd just eaten lying heavily in my stomach. I shifted the carrier bag and watched as people got on and off the bus. I looked at them. I wondered where they were going once they'd left the bus and I wondered if I could still fly.

In bed, I lay still, my hands flat on either side of me and I breathed deeply, in and out. I was waiting. I'd put on a tracksuit, a dark blue one that had been at the bottom of my wardrobe. I thought a tracksuit was appropriate for night time flying.

Outside it was dark, inside my bedside lamp was on, its light pooled on the small unit next to my bed. I closed my eyes.

At first, I didn't realise it had happened again. I didn't think I'd fallen asleep but, somehow, without me feeling it, I'd risen at least three feet from the bed. I felt a surge of excitement. I'd done it again, I was floating.

This time I concentrated on what I was feeling. I felt light, buoyant, the heaviness in my body had seeped away. I was as light as air. I laughed out loud, the feeling was exhilarating.

I floated out of the bedroom, into the living room. I looked at my sofa, I'd been watching a film, *The Lady in the Van*, as Dan had recommended it. I saw the sag in the sofa where I'd been sitting. I floated out into the hallway towards the front door. I saw the square of coloured glass in the door. I saw the amber glow of a street light through the glass. It seemed improbable, risky, but the thought was lodged in my mind: "Could I fly outside?"

I eased myself towards the door. I'd worked out how to move: all I had to do was hold my head up. It was that easy. I opened the door. My heart was hammering, and my mouth was dry. It was quiet outside. No one walked past, no dog walker, no car returning home from a late night. I took a deep breath and, closing the door behind me, I left my home.

I felt empowered; the knowledge, the *understanding* of what I alone could do, was heady. I floated towards a garden, above straggly conifer trees. I flew over a rotary clothes line. In the moonlight, it looked like a silvery spider's web. A bird flew past, I heard its confused cheep. I swooped, I dived, I held my arms out. I could fly.

I moved away from the street, I flew across the river. I saw boats moored near the bank, I saw how they bobbed up and down as the water moved. I wondered what it would be like to feel that movement when you slept.

I hovered, like a hawk, in the night air. Dan lived close by. I knew his address. I knew it as if my mum had sewn it into my clothes, like the labels she'd sewn into my school uniform: 52, Greenfield Avenue.

I thought about it, seeing Dan's house, seeing where he lived with Nina and the girls. I lifted my head, my body moved, it was instinctive.

Greenfield Avenue was a long road, flanked by plane trees. I saw no one and I moved between the trees, feeling the large leaves touch my hands, my face. I couldn't see any numbers. I didn't know which one was Dan's. I knew I had to get closer, *fly* closer. The thought both terrified and excited me.

I glanced up and down the road. No one was around. I took a deep breath and dropped. I moved closer to the houses. I'd flown this far and I promised myself I'd simply see Dan's house. That would be enough, for now.

I lifted my arms, I flew higher and I moved slowly, trying to gauge where Dan's house might be. There, down there, number 52. It was a detached house. I remembered Dan talking about his house, about the wreck it had been when he bought it. I moved towards his home. Two bay trees stood in pots on either side of the front door. They were guarding the house, like sentries with glossy green leaves.

Now I'd found it, I wasn't sure what I wanted to do. The house, like all its neighbours, was in darkness. Or was it? There was a gap in the curtains in an upstairs window, a tiny sliver of light amidst the darkness. My heart was beating so fast that it frightened me. I looked up and down the road again. There was nothing, just the wind moving through the enormous plane trees. Almost without my realising it, my body floated towards the sliver of light.

The beating of my heart had become a deafening roar. I took a deep breath, willing my heart rate to slow and then I moved inch by inch towards the window. I grabbed the windowsill and I peered in. I saw a bed, a shape on the bed. A head, hair flattened on the pillow. It was Nina, Dan's wife. She was lying curled up, facing the window, her eyes were closed. There was no sign of Dan. I watched her for a moment, looking at her face, the smoothness of her skin. I shifted, the movement sent my body floating again. I flew over the roof of Dan's house. I saw the back garden, the fence that separated one garden from its neighbours. I dropped slowly, noiselessly. I made a silent promise: one more view of Dan's house and then I'd go home. That would be enough for one night.

As I floated ever closer to the downstairs rooms, a security light flashed on. I held my breath. I steadied myself, my arms at my sides. The light remained on for a few seconds then gradually faded and I breathed out.

My feet were almost on the ground, a shadowy blue light shone through the French doors. I saw Dan, his back to me and he was sitting in front of a computer screen. His hand covered the mouse, an empty wine glass was nearby.

I watched him, I looked at the way he slouched in the chair, his shoulders sagged, his head was still.

A dog barked. It sounded close by. I froze, my eyes on Dan. I heard the sound of paws scrabbling at a fence. I rose, I left Dan's house. I flew home, with the images I'd seen stored in my head, to keep them, to relive them.

In the office the next day, I heard Dan say that he and Nina had sat up until the early hours talking about a film they'd seen. I heard the way he spoke, firmly, as if he was emphasising the point. I didn't say a word. How could I?

I knew I'd go again.

Once more, there was a gap in the curtains and, once more I saw Nina. She was sitting up in bed, a handkerchief balled in her fist, her eyes red-rimmed. I didn't stay long and I floated towards the back of the house.

I saw a thin line of light from a back bedroom window. That's where I saw him, Dan, lying on his back on a single bed, his bare feet sticking out from underneath a duvet. The duvet had Harry Potter's face on the cover. The next morning, he told the office he'd spent the evening painting the living room. "Nina's been on my case for ages."

Why did no one else see the shadows under Dan's eyes, or see the slump of his shoulders?

At home, getting ready to go to work, I practised saying, "Is everything all right? Is there anything I can do to help?" I watched in the mirror as I spoke, looking at the way my mouth formed the words. I dressed carefully: a loose, black tunic skimming my hips, elastic-waisted trousers, falling in soft folds, the buckles on my shoes glinting.

Lunchtime, I walked to Dan's desk where he sat hunched over his computer. I cleared my throat, "Dan, is everything all right? You seem a little down." I swallowed, I kept my voice low, "Is there anything I can do?"

He glanced at me, "No, thank you, Cassie. Everything's fine."

My rehearsed words hung in the air and Dan looked away. I stood for a moment, looking at the way his hair curled over the collar of his shirt.

I moved away. I bumped into Sarah who held two packets of sandwiches and I saw how she tumbled them into Dan's lap. I returned to my desk and I watched as Sarah put her head close to Dan's. I heard her laughter, I saw Sarah lift her head, she caught my eye. I saw the smile on her face, there was more than mockery in her eyes, she was gloating.

Later, when everyone had gone home, I went through Sarah's file. I looked at her address: 21a, Ladymead Road.

There were no clouds that night, an array of stars twinkled and I felt a surge of adrenaline as I flew over roofs, soared over the neat lines of back gardens, the swings and slides empty on the night-darkened lawns.

When I arrived at Ladymead Road, I hesitated, swooping low over privet hedges, looking for number 21a. An illuminated panel told me that Sarah's flat was on the top floor. I powered my way upwards, towards Sarah.

At the top of the building, Sarah obviously knew that she wasn't overlooked and light streamed from a large window. I floated towards the windowsill and I peered in. There was no sign of Sarah. I heard music, a rhythmic beat, it might have been *Coldplay*. Three mismatched chairs were grouped around a fireplace. A bookcase held a line of paperbacks and a dusty spider plant. The walls were bare, there were no prints, no photographs. I sniffed, I didn't think it was much of a place. I thought about my flat, my yellow chair, my IKEA sofa.

Then Sarah appeared. My fingers tightened on the sill, I pulled myself closer.

She was holding a blue mug, a spiral of steam rose and she settled into an armchair. She was wearing pyjamas, I recognised the pattern. She'd bought them in Marks and Spencer, I had a pair just like them.

Her head lifted, she saw me. I saw the confusion in her eyes, I saw how her mouth opened. I let go of the sill and floated upward. She had an uninterrupted view of my body, dressed in a dark blue track suit, hovering in front of her top floor window. I smiled and lifted one hand to wave at her. Then I floated away. I heard her scream.

I wondered what she'd say to Dan in the morning.

Dancing at the Bay

The girls always arrived first, a gaggle of teenagers, their voices high with excitement, petticoats rustling, heels clip-clopping on the planks of wood that ran the length of the pier. They were going to the Bay, a squat, timber-framed building standing at the end of the pier. They went every week to the dance held there. As soon as they had paid their entrance money, they trooped off to the Ladies to check their appearance. It never seemed to matter that they'd already spent hours getting ready.

The glitter ball revolved, its light briefly flickering into the empty corners of the Bay. The band played listlessly, the singer pleading, "Come on, who's going to be the first up on the floor?" No one wanted to be the first, the girls waited for the boys to arrive and the boys were assessing the girls.

For Christine, it was a weekly disappointment. She came every Saturday with her best friend, Lynda. Christine was sixteen years old and each week she thought that things would be different: she'd meet someone, someone would ask her to dance, he'd hold her hand, would bend his head towards her, listening to what she had to say.

That hadn't happened, what *did* happen was that two boys would approach Christine and Lynda. Christine usually saw them first, she'd see the nudges, the face pulling, the boy who had eyes for Lynda had to coerce his mate into asking Christine for a dance. The boy would mumble, they always mumbled and Christine would smile her acceptance, then the four of them would troop out to the centre of the dance floor. Each week, Christine tried talking to her partner, but the response was usually a nod, the boy's eyes focusing on something over Christine's shoulder. As soon as the music had finished, there might be a grunt, it could signify "thanks" or it might simply mean relief that the boy (she never knew their names) could go back to the other side of the room.

After that, Christine would sit on one of the hard wooden chairs that lined the walls of the dance floor and she'd watch Lynda as she giggled and flirted with the boy she was dancing with.

When she watched Lynda, Christine often thought of how they got ready for the dance, the way they cut lemons in half, squeezing the juice on to the top of their heads before rushing out to the garden, hoping the sunshine would last long enough to bleach the sticky strands of hair.

Christine thought of the careful way she ironed her dress and the new packet of *American Tan* stockings she bought each week; she thought of the hours she spent lying in the bath, trying not to smile as the face pack splintered around her mouth and eyes.

Christine watched Lynda, looking at the way she moved inside her cotton dress, the way the patterned shirtwaister skimmed her narrow hips. She saw how the boy's hand rested on her friend's tiny waist. Christine believed that Lynda knew far more about the art of boys simply because she was slim, that she had an insight into the way their minds worked.

Christine tugged unhappily at the front of her dress. She'd bought it in C&A, saving up for it, putting five shillings a week into her Post Office account. Her mother said the cost of clothes was a scandal, "I could make four for that price." Christine didn't want a home-made dress. Being overweight *and* wearing a dress that her mother had made; if that happened, she might as well stay at home.

From where she sat, Christine could see the boys, she watched as their heads swung towards the door when another group of boys sauntered in. Some were chewing gum, hands in their pockets as they joined the crowd scattered around the door.

She saw the way they pushed each other, their smiles taking away any aggression. She saw heads lowered as they compared notes, she saw the way their eyes roamed over the girls, sometimes a finger would point, then there'd be more nudging before a boy, determinedly casual, wandered over to the girls.

Rarely did a boy look in her direction. If a boy did look, his eyes slid away, the glance barely registering. Christine wasn't the only girl sitting on the chairs. There was Valerie who wore National Health glasses, there was Margaret whose face was covered in a forest of acne; there was Susan, who wore the same red dress every week and left a peculiar smell in her wake and there was Jenni who always brought a book to read. *We're sort of a gang, a gang of leftovers*, thought Christine.

She always told her parents that she had a great time at the Bay. "It's mad there, non-stop dancing." She liked their indulgent smiles. Sometimes, they waited up for her, opening the front door when Lynda's Dad brought them home in his Ford Prefect. She listened to the way they spoke to Lynda's father. "These youngsters, they don't know they're born, do they?"

Lynda had been forbidden to go home with any of the boys she met. "Same goes for you too, Christine," said her father. Christine nodded, her eyebrows raised to express exasperation.

On Monday, she went to school. She heard all about Pamela Evans who'd gone "all the way" with the boy she'd met for the first time on Friday night. In the lunch break, Christine watched as Pamela was surrounded by girls, all desperate to know what 'it' had been like. She saw the way Pamela tucked her hair behind her ears before giving everyone a sheepish smile.

Lynda said she wanted to leave school at the end of the summer term. "What's the point of staying on? I can get a good job anywhere. I can easily earn £5 a week."

Christine told her parents what Lynda had said. She spoke rapidly, as if she was dropping the idea into their laps.

"But I thought you wanted to take A-levels," her mother said.

"I do," Christine agreed, relieved because somehow the decision had been made for her.

She also told her mother that she wanted to lose weight. "Whatever for?" her mother asked, plunging her hands into soapy dishwater, "You're big-boned, that's all, you take after me, didn't put your father off."

Christine knew all about how her parents met. She knew that her father, home on leave from the RAF saw her mother at a dance. "I was with my mates, your father was with his." It had been the precision of it, the quiet acceptance that had always bothered Christine.

When her mother said, "See, our mates married each other, we thought we might as well do the same," she glanced at Christine's father as if daring him to make a comment. He kept quiet, his head bent low over his supper of fish and chips.

Christine persisted with her plan to go on a diet. She heard her mother tell her father, "She's alright as she is."

"I like to see a girl with meat on her bones," her father replied.

Christine pulled a face and the next day, at the tea table, she ate her salad: tired lettuce leaves adorned with slices of hardboiled egg and soggy tomatoes, she shook her head when her mother asked if she wanted salad cream.

She was presented with the identical salad each mealtime. Her father teased her, "Got your eye on some boy then, have you?"

Christine blushed, "No." She knew her father would assume

27

she meant "Yes".

On Friday, Lynda sat next to her in the dining hall. They wore the same uniform, navy pleated skirt and a white shirt with a yellow and navy tie. Lynda managed to look both sexy and neat in hers. Christine was aware that the pleats in her skirt bunched up around her waist, making her look larger than ever.

"All right for tomorrow?" Lynda asked, her fork digging into the pile of mashed potato on her plate.

"I'm not sure..." Christine began.

"Oh, come on. We always have a laugh, what else are you going to do?"

Christine shrugged, what else would she do? She'd only be watching television with her parents. She agreed to meet Lynda at her house where they could get ready together.

They washed their petticoats, sloshing sugared water along the delicate lace hems. They hung them on the line, watching idly as wasps buzzed around the petticoats, flapping in the summer breeze.

They took it in turns to shave each other's legs; massaging Lynda's mother's Pond's cream into their reddened skin. Lynda's hair was long and dark blonde; she piled it on top of her head, turning from left to right as she fastened earrings borrowed from her sister.

Christine's hair was unruly: it grew in thick curls that escaped all the clips she shoved in. It would be a waste of time putting earrings in, as her hair covered everything. She knew that the lemon juice they used added pale gold highlights to Lynda's hair, but made no difference to Christine's rusty red curls.

She dressed in the bathroom, not wanting Lynda to see the mounds of flesh as she tugged her dress over her hips. She sighed, a week of lettuce and boiled eggs hadn't made much difference. She heard the rasp of nylon as her thighs rubbed together and she slipped her feet into the sling-backed shoes she kept for Saturday nights.

Lynda's Dad, "Call me Trev," drove them towards the pier, telling them not to do anything he wouldn't do before dropping them off on his way to the Conservative club.

There were only four other girls inside the Bay when they arrived. Christine waved before she and Lynda made their way to the Ladies. Each time, as she stood next to Lynda, staring into the rust-spotted mirror, Christine held her breath. From the moment she left the house to the time she arrived at the Bay, she hoped there might have been a change, that somehow, miraculously, her appearance might have altered and instead of the full cheeked face and wayward curls, she'd see a reflection of a girl with defined cheekbones and obedient hair. It had never happened, she always looked the same. She sighed and Lynda undid the top button of her lace blouse and Christine tugged unhappily at the front of her dress. She ran a finger over her teeth in case her new, red lipstick had strayed.

"Ready?" Lynda asked, her hand on the door. Christine nodded and they made their way over to the other girls.

There was a group of boys near the door as Lynda and Christine walked across the dance floor. Someone whistled and Lynda half-turned, one hand patting at her lacquered hair. Christine knew that Lynda assumed the wolf whistle was for her; not for one second did she think it might have been meant for Christine. The band launched into their version of *Wake Up Little Susie* and the girls tapped their feet. Christine watched the glitter ball as it twinkled its way around the walls.

"Want to dance?" For a second, she remained still until Lynda nudged her.

Turning, she saw him. He was tall and he wore a blue suit, his shirt was white and the knot in his dark red tie almost reached his Adam's apple.

"Me?" Christine put a hand to her chest, "Are you asking me?"

The boy nodded, his face reddening.

"But no-one's on the floor yet." Christine felt flustered.

"That means we'll be the first." He stood to one side and, conscious of the eyes of the other girls, Christine walked to the middle of the dance floor.

Knowing that Lynda would be watching, Christine mouthed the words to the song, she kept her head turned, hoping that Lynda would think she was talking. She risked a quick glance at her friend and she gave a nervous smile as Lynda gave her a thumbs up. Taking a deep breath, Christine looked at the boy's face. She was startled to see that he'd been watching her. She blushed, hating the fact that her neck would soon become a mottled red. She gave him a nervous smile before lowering her gaze.

"What's your name?" the boy bent towards her.

"What, pardon?" she stammered.

"Your name, what's your name?"

"Christine," she said it quickly, lifting her head for a second.

"I'm Peter," his head was lowered, close to her face. "I've seen you here before, you always come in with your friend, the blonde one."

"Lynda, yes, we come most weeks."

Christine found it hard to concentrate on her dancing, she wanted Peter to continue talking to her, but she also wanted the other girls to see him talking. She glanced over at the chairs, checking to see who was sitting there. She saw Jenni, her head bent low over a book. For the first time, Christine wondered how she could see to read in the half-light. The others were there:

30

Valerie sat next to Margaret, Susan was a few feet away. Christine felt a sudden rush of excitement, *I'm not in the left-over gang, I'm dancing with a boy*.

Peter said something.

"Sorry?" Christine stepped closer and he closed his hand over hers.

"I said I like your hair, it looks natural, not stiff with lacquer." He spoke in a rush, the words hurtling from his mouth. It sounded, Christine thought, as if he'd forced them out, as if he'd been keeping them in his head and wanted to say them quickly.

"Thank you."

Peter's hand still held hers, and as the band stopped playing, he tugged her wrist, pulling her closer. She stood quietly, in an agony of hope that he wouldn't simply mutter "thanks" and bolt over to rejoin his mates. Instead, he asked if she'd like a drink. A refreshment table stood at the far end of the dance floor, with long necked bottles of *Tizer, Dandelion and Burdock* huddled together and a plastic tray for coins held a few coppers. Christine nodded and, still holding her hand, Peter shepherded her towards the table.

The band started up again and the singer, standing so close to the microphone that his asthmatic wheezes could be heard, introduced another Everly Brothers song, *Walk Right Back*. Christine saw the glint of blonde as Lynda moved to the middle of the dance floor.

Peter handed her a bottle of *Tizer* and, in silence, they watched the dancers, their mouths sucking on long, white straws. "That girl, your mate, do you always come with her?" Peter's head jerked in Lynda's direction.

"Yes, she's my best friend, we're in the same class at school." Christine felt her heart lurch, as she thought she understood why Peter had asked her to dance. He just wanted to get closer to

31

Lynda. But Peter was looking at Christine, with a smile on his face.

"I'm staying on for my A levels, are you?"

She nodded, relief seeping through her, "Yes, I am."

Peter led her back to the dance floor as the singer began his version of *Lucille*.

She sat in the back of Lynda's Dad's car, half-listening to their bickering. "All I'm saying, Lynda, is that you should think about it, that's all."

Lynda sighed, "Not this again, Dad. I've made up my mind, I'm leaving school. You were the one who said if I could type I'd always find work."

Christine heard the regret in Lynda's father's voice. "That's not quite what I meant. Why don't you do what Christine's doing, staying on?"

Christine sat quietly, registering the fact that Lynda had remained silent. She wanted to say Peter's name, to speak it aloud. She relived every moment, from the time he asked her to dance, to the moment he kissed her. Christine squirmed when she thought about the kiss. Her first time and she got it wrong. Her nose had collided with his and, just as she whispered, "Sorry," his mouth landed on hers. She'd opened her eyes to find herself staring into Peter's eyes. She saw his eyes widen before she closed hers.

He wanted to see her again, "Will you be here next week?"

Christine nodded happily, "Yes, I will."

Lynda had danced every dance. Christine had seen her friend's skirt swirling around her knees as she jived.

Turning away from her father, Lynda asked, "Did you have a good time?"

Christine nodded, suddenly shy, "Yes, I did. He wants to know if I'm going next week."

"Who wants to know?"

The boy I was with," Christine lifted her head to say his name, "Peter."

Lynda turned away, "Yeah, they all say that. It's a cheap date for them."

Christine shook her head, then realised nobody could see her. "He's not like that," she spoke softly.

That night, at home in her bedroom, Christine kicked off the pale pink eiderdown and stared into the darkness. She whispered, "Peter". She smiled.

After meeting Peter, Christine spent the week agonising over what to wear, she tried on almost everything she had in her wardrobe, she spent pocket money on Miners block mascara, on pearly pink nail varnish. At home, sitting up in bed, she wrote *Peter* on notebooks, she wrote it on the back of her hand, washing it off before her parents saw it. She pleaded with her mother to let her dye her hair blonde. "Over my dead body," her mother said. "Most people would give their eye teeth to have hair like yours."

Christine endured another week of limp salads and, on Saturday afternoon, she and Lynda locked themselves in Christine's bedroom to begin their preparations.

Lynda had tried to straighten Christine's hair; she'd read that ironing hair would take out the curl. Ignoring Christine's mother's raised eyebrow, they put the ironing board up in Christine's room and, sitting close to the iron, Lynda yanked at Christine's hair, trying to get it flat so she could iron it. It didn't work, her hair remained curly and the smell of scorched hair filtered through the house.

Then it was time to go and they linked arms as they walked into the Bay.

Christine's heart was thumping, she looked straight ahead,

forcing herself not to look for Peter. She sent unspoken prayers, *Please let him be here, I'll do the dishes for a month.* She followed Lynda into the Ladies, her eyes glued to the back of her friend's head.

When they came out, Peter was standing outside. Christine was so glad to see him, to know that he'd turned up, she stopped suddenly and Lynda cannoned into her.

Christine had to fight the impulse to say, "You came, you came." Instead she smiled nervously as Peter reached for her hand. She saw Lynda give Peter a cursory glance and, when he gave her a brief smile, her friend moved away, walking over to the other girls. Christine walked with Peter to the centre of the dance floor.

She stayed with him for the whole evening. They danced for most of the time and, at 10.30, when the band was playing Are *You Lonesome Tonight?* Peter held her close, she felt his finger tugging gently on her curls. Lynda was dancing close by, she mimed a yawn when she caught Christine's eye. For a second, a tiny second, Christine thought about doing the same, pretending that she too was bored, but she didn't. Instead she closed her eyes and put her head on Peter's shoulder.

Peter wanted to walk her home, "I've brought my bike, I can walk to your house then get on my bike to go home."

She stared at his face, looking for…she wasn't sure what she was looking for. Was he an axe murderer? Would he drag her off into the bushes? At that point, her imagination stalled. She gave him a nervous smile, "I usually go home with my friend's father, he picks us up in his car."

"Please? I'd like to take you home."

Christine was in an agony of indecision. She wanted to go home with Peter, to walk with him through the quiet streets, to listen to his voice telling her of his plans, of the university he wanted to attend and just to be with him.

Lynda touched her arm, "Are you ready? Dad's outside, he says to get a move on."

Christine looked at her friend; she saw how the sparkly blue eye shadow had smudged under Lynda's eyes, blonde hair had escaped from the clips and slides, wispy strands trailed to Lynda's shoulders. She shook her head, "No, I'm walking home with Peter."

She saw the shock in Lynda's eyes, "But you can't, your Mum and Dad will go mad, they told you to come home with me."

Christine looked at her friend, "Not tonight, I'm walking home."

Lynda shook her head, "You'll be in so much trouble." She walked away, her shoulders high with indignation.

Christine forgot about Lynda, she forgot about her parents, she was only aware of Peter. With one hand he held his bike and with the other he gripped Christine's hand. He held on so tightly, her fingers felt crushed, but she ignored the discomfort and concentrated on Peter's words instead. He went to school in a boys' only grammar school, he told her about his brother, "He's at Manchester University, he wants to be a doctor." He told her about his parents, they were both teachers. As she listened, Christine pictured his family: she saw them in a large detached house, manicured lawns and beds of roses. There was a dining room with dark oak furniture, rugs on the parquet floor, pictures on the walls, shelves lined with books. When Peter asked about her parents, Christine said, "They're just ordinary, Dad works as a printer and Mum stays at home." She felt a momentary pang of disloyalty.

When they reached her house, Christine had a sense of being watched; she looked up at the windows: the curtains were drawn, the house was in darkness, only the porch light shone and she had strict instructions to switch it off as soon as she opened the front door. She had the distinct feeling that her parents were lying in bed, ears strained, listening for the sound of her coming home.

Peter propped his bike up against the privet hedge, he turned towards her and this time Christine got it right, she closed her eyes as she waited for his kiss.

On Monday, when Christine arrived at school, she was aware of the glances from the other girls: they smiled at her, they jostled to sit next to her, they nudged her, "So, what's he like? Is he your boyfriend?"

Feeling flustered, Christine stammered, "He just walked me home, that's all."

"Did he kiss you? What's his kissing like?"

Christine shrugged, "OK," she wondered what she had to compare it with. She'd never kissed a boy before. She looked around to see where Lynda was. They normally sat together in lessons. Lynda was coming through the classroom door. She waved when she saw Christine, and the other girls moved away, allowing Lynda to sit next to Christine.

"You OK?" Lynda asked, putting her books on the desk.

Suddenly shy, Christine nodded. "Yes, I'm fine." The class fell silent as Miss Hughes, the Latin teacher, came into the room.

At lunchtime, Christine was once again the centre of attention. "What's his name? Are you seeing him again?"

"His name's Peter and we're going to the pictures on Thursday." As soon as the words left her mouth, Christine wanted to claw them back. It felt wrong, telling the others about Peter. Being with him was too new, too fragile to share with anyone else. What if he didn't turn up? What if she never saw him again?"

Looking at the girls, their faces turned towards her, Christine knew that she'd only ever been Lynda's big friend, of no special interest. Now that a boy had taken her home, she was in the spotlight and she didn't feel comfortable.

She looked mutely towards Lynda. Her friend shrugged, "Don't know what all the fuss is about. He's only a boy."

Her words had the effect of cold water, of dampening down the girls' interest, of quelling Christine's excitement. The girls turned their attention to their plates of food and Christine saw how their eyes flicked towards Lynda, listening to her tales of the dances she'd had, "You should see the blister on my heel, I didn't sit down once all night."

Christine felt the wave of interest in her drain away, she chewed doggedly on a piece of overcooked beef and smiled at Lynda's description of a boy she'd danced with. "Honest to God, you should have heard him, all he talked about was his motorbike." The girls all laughed, a light laugh. None of them had Lynda's looks, none of them danced as much as she did. None of them had her insouciance, her confidence that there would always be a boy wanting to dance with her.

During the rest of the school day, Christine opened her mouth a few times to tell Lynda about Peter, to tell her about the way he looked at her, listening to every word she spoke, but somehow there hadn't been the right time.

At home, her parents teased her, "So, when are we going to meet your young man?"

"He's not my young man, he's just Peter, someone I met." She yearned to leave the table, their smiles, their *ordinariness*, to escape to her bedroom where she could think about him.

He said he'd meet her outside the Odeon to see *Dr. Zhivago*. She told her Mum that she'd be out of the house by 7 o'clock. "Can we have tea a bit earlier?"

"Suppose we can," her mother said. Her smile was arch, it

made Christine's teeth ache.

On Thursday, Christine was presented with another plate of salad. Her mother brought it to the table as if it was a trophy. "Bought the lettuce in the market, went specially for you," she said. Idly, Christine wondered if her mother thought that the lettuce had magical powers. She thanked her and gulped down her meal.

She was too early, there was no one outside the Odeon. She'd got off the bus and had walked slowly, listening to the thud of her heels as she made her way to the cinema, but there was no sign of Peter. Telling herself it would be OK, that he would turn up, Christine walked around the block, she stared in shop windows, she loitered in front of Clarks' shoe shop, willing her heart to stop thumping. Glancing at her watch, she made her way slowly back to the Odeon. He was there!

Feeling suddenly shy, Christine touched his arm, and he turned and smiled at her.

It didn't take long for Christine to realise that there were now two parts to her life. There was the time she spent with Peter, sitting in the cinema, holding hands, talking about the films they'd seen, walking to the beach, drinking coffee in a noisy café and dancing with him at the Bay. She kept her time with Peter to herself, not wanting to spoil or risk anything by telling either Lynda or her parents. There was the other part where she went to school, she sat through lessons, she talked to Lynda, she went home, she ate her meals with her parents and then she went to bed, lying underneath the heavy pink eiderdown.

Dancing at the Bay was different, she had to admit that. She still went with Lynda, but she met Peter outside. They went in together with Lynda trailing behind. Christine didn't walk to the Ladies with Lynda, instead she moved across the dance floor to sit with

Peter on the hard-backed chairs, listening to the band.

Sometimes she'd watch Lynda making her way across the floor, looking at her friend, thinking of the preparations they'd made. They still met at each other's houses, they still laughed together as their face packs splintered, or squirmed as the rivulets of lemon juice trickled down their necks. Christine didn't get dressed in the bathroom any longer. Maybe it had been the lettuce bought at the market, maybe it had been the dances she did with Peter, but her clothes were loose, she didn't pluck at the front of her dresses, she didn't hear the rasp of nylon when she put on her stockings.

She'd watch Lynda walk over to the other girls, she saw the way her friend moved, understanding that Lynda knew that all eyes were on her. She'd hear the squeals of laughter from the girls, she'd see the way the glitterball lit up the blonde in Lynda's hair, how it touched Valerie's glasses before moving on. She sat holding Peter's hand as they listened to the band, hearing the singer plead for someone to start dancing. She saw two boys saunter over to Lynda, she saw one of the boys touch Lynda's arm, making her turn towards him. She saw the other boy touch Margaret's arm. She watched the two girls, boys in tow, move towards the centre of the dance floor.

She heard Peter, "Do you want to dance?" She nodded and they too walked to the centre of the dance floor.

I Thought It Was You

The waiter, shoes squeaking on the tiled floor, had shown us to a window table. My husband had booked that particular table, knowing I liked the view of the river. We had the usual question, "Would you like to see the wine list, sir?" and we sat there for a while, enjoying the view, the atmosphere. Neither of us looked at the menu, at least not immediately. We're regulars and, after over thirty years of marriage, we know each other's tastes.

The waiter appeared again, a bottle of Sancerre in one hand, an ice bucket in the other. Again, the ritual, this time, of tasting the wine. My husband swirled the wine in his glass, took a sip and, nodding, told the waiter it was fine.

We toasted each other, "Happy Anniversary." We smiled.

I picked up the menu and then I saw you. You were by the door, a woman at your side. A waiter was checking the bookings, you said something to the woman and, when you turned, you saw me too.

It's been a long time, nearly forty years and I thought it was you. Is it you? Your hair is still too long and it's no longer blond. It's a silvery white, curling as it always did, on the collar of the jacket you wore, a dark cream, linen jacket. My husband won't wear linen, he says it creases and doesn't look right.

You looked at me as if you couldn't work out if, indeed, it was me. I felt like that too. I wanted to smile, to wave, but I didn't and neither did you. The moment passed and the waiter escorted you to your table. I watched as you went by.

My husband asked if I knew what I wanted to order. He said he'd bet I'd order the sea bass. I laughed, I always laughed. I told him he knew me too well. Without turning my head, I saw the waiter hold the chair out for your companion; is she your wife?

It's easier to order the sea-bass, it's expected. My husband and I spoke about our son and his wife, and the new baby due in six weeks' time. We talked about taking a short break before the baby arrives, knowing we'll be needed, just like before when our granddaughter was born. We talk easily and if our conversation doesn't exactly flow, it's not forced or stilted either. I'm aware, in the periphery of my vision, that the woman you're with has stretched out her hand to take yours. Did I imagine it or was there an almost imperceptible hesitation on your part? On the pretext of gazing at the other diners, I turn to look at you. Your hands are the same: long-fingered with blunt, square shaped nails. You look up. There's a question in your eyes. What? What is it? What are you asking? I can't tell.

It was never easy to read you.

I was seventeen when we met. It's odd, but something has shifted, and now I can see what I wore that day. I was going to an interview and I've not thought about that for years, and yet I remember the dark blue skirt, the blindingly white blouse and the plain leather shoes I wore. My mother had ironed the blouse, putting starch into the collar and it rubbed against my neck. She said I needed to look the part for an interview.

I got the job, but you know that. To be a trainee reporter was all I'd ever dreamt about. One of the first things I remember about you was the laughter in your eyes. I felt hurt, sure that you were mocking me, a gauche teenager, wearing clothes far too old for her years.

There were eight years between us, but at first, there might as well have been forty. You had a job title: *Motoring Correspondent.* You wouldn't wear a suit, preferring a battered leather jacket which creaked when you moved. I always knew where you were in the newsroom because of that jacket.

You singled me out. I didn't understand. Why me? I was nervous, inept, a girl who blushed easily, whose hair was uncontrollable, who went home each night to her parents and her childhood bedroom. Eight years, that was all, and yet you were assured, confident and, bewilderingly, you seemed to like my company.

We went out on stories together, you with your notebook, your commanding presence and me. All I did at first was tag along behind you, hoping that my shorthand was as good as I'd been told by my teacher. Somehow, I improved, my confidence grew and, when I was asked to cover a story on my own, you were the first person I told. Again, your eyes were full of humour and it confused me. What had I been expecting? Praise? Recognition? All you said was that you knew I could do it. I hadn't known that.

You were there the whole time. If I did well, if a story of mine made it to the front page, you were the first person I wanted to tell. Then, one day, not long after my birthday, you asked me out. It confused me, was it a date? All you did was smile and tell me about the restaurant you'd chosen.

I can remember the agony of trying to choose what to wear. What sort of restaurant was it? My family were not big on fancy restaurants, so I had no experience of them. My mother didn't understand my concern about what to wear. She said that people shouldn't be judged by appearance. I reminded her how she'd insisted on me wearing a white blouse to the interview. She said that was different.

In the end, I borrowed a blouse from her and wore a pleated

skirt, one that I'd bought with my first week's wages. I polished my shoes and made sure that I had a handkerchief in my handbag, something else my Mum was big on.

The restaurant had been busy. Waiters weaved their way around the tables. You told me people went there because of the fish, it was always fresh. I'd never thought about that before.

Whenever I went out with my Mum and Dad, we went because my Mum said it was a treat for her, not having to cook. Now that I think about it, the restaurant was like this one, full of appreciative diners, white table linen and silver buckets of wine.

The sea bass has arrived. My husband ordered it too. He often does that. We discussed a holiday later in the year. We are going to France, we like it there. My husband always says there'll be no nasty surprises. There is that. The fish is good, it usually is and for a while, we eat in silence. It's not an uncomfortable silence, merely a quiet time.

It's odd, the feeling that you're close by. I'm aware of you. It might be that you're looking at me, I don't know.

Our date, because that's what it was, was the first of many. You encouraged me to learn to drive, you were waiting when the test had finished and I told you I'd passed. You said you hadn't doubted it for one minute. I had. When I was with you, I understood for the first time, that I could achieve anything I wanted. You'd asked me why I hadn't chosen university after leaving school. It was no-one's fault. I tried to explain that it was something that my family didn't do. I made a joke, telling you my Dad had viewed it in the same light as if I'd announced I wanted to become a Tibetan monk. It was a world he knew nothing about. You said that wasn't fair, you said I should learn to make my own decisions.

When you told me that a London newspaper had offered you a

contract, one you didn't want to refuse, at first I didn't understand what you were saying. London was another world I knew nothing about. It was when you said that you would live there, I understood then. We'd gone back to the restaurant, the first one, and you'd leant across the table to take my hand and told me you wanted me to come with you, to move to London. You told me it was everything you'd ever wanted and I saw the excitement in your eyes.

All I could think about was leaving my home. I couldn't get past that. I tried, I did try, but London took on the shape of a boulder. It blocked everything. My parents had only ever lived in the same town, holidays had been trips to Cornwall, same caravan, same week every year. Did I want that? I didn't think so, but I didn't know what else I wanted either.

You told me you had to leave, the job wouldn't wait and I was too frightened to make a decision. So you went. You sent postcards of Buckingham Palace, of Regents' Park, of all the places I'd only ever heard about. On each card was a question mark. I knew what you were asking, yet I didn't know what the answer was. Then the cards stopped.

What is it about life, how it closes over and smooths things out? I didn't forget about you, but you weren't *there*.

I became chief reporter, first time a woman had held that position and I wanted to tell you, but I couldn't. I remembered what you said, about being able to achieve anything I wanted.

I got married, my children arrived and, although I still worked, I knew something was missing. Something I hadn't done. It's easy to talk about a piece of the jigsaw missing, but that's how it felt. My picture was almost complete.

I applied for a place at university. What would you have said about that?

I smile and have to turn away in case my husband asks what is so funny. I smile because I knew you'd have said, "What took you so long?"

We're here today because it's our wedding anniversary and I'm wearing pearls. I touch them, feeling their satiny smoothness. They're a present from my husband. He says I should have nice things.

I turn, just to get another look at you. Your companion is sitting back, her eyes on your face. It's an expression I recognise, she's trying to work out what is going on. What are you saying to her?

I graduated and my family was there to celebrate and it was another wonderful day to add to our memories. My life has been good, it's been successful in a lot of ways. One word to describe it? "Constant". It followed a path: no peaks, no troughs. So what am I saying? Has my life been boring? No, not that. And yet it's been without any real anxieties or upheavals. Surely that's what most of us want, isn't it? A life without drama, running on smooth lines. As we grow older, we're sure of ourselves and those around us. Isn't that what most people want? Isn't it?

My husband asks if I want dessert. He teases me, his usual joke about my love of crème caramel and I give in, just like he knew I would.

I hear the harsh squeak of a chair and I turn. The woman you're with, she's standing. Her face is flushed and her eyes are glassy. She brushes past my chair and I can smell her perfume, it's not one I recognise.

My husband pulls a face and asks what that was all about.

I hear your voice asking for the bill.

I still don't know if it's you. It might be.

Our desserts have arrived and I see a waiter putting your bill on the table. My husband talks about whether we need to replace the carpet in our bedroom.

Once more, I half-turn and watch you leave the table. I look at you and, as you move away, I catch your eye. There, it is you. You smile, but I don't know if you've recognised me, or whether you feel I'm someone you might have known…someone whose face is familiar but you're not sure why.

Plate Juggling

I know it's her. I can hear her. Those awful shoes she wears, what are they called? *Crocs?* They look nothing like crocodiles, they look like plastic pasties. Anyway, they make a noise, they squeak. Don't know how she manages that. Every floor in this place is carpeted, but I can hear her coming. It shouldn't bother me, but it does.

Her name is Kirsty. Doesn't suit her. It might have suited her when she was younger but not now. She's probably in her late fifties, though she could be older. She looks as if she's carrying the weight of the world on her shoulders. Maybe working here has stripped her of the ability to smile. I can understand that.

Here she is, a trolley in front of her, dishing out cups of tea and *Rich Tea* biscuits. We only get two and I could murder a *Jaffa Cake*, but they're not allowed apparently. Life here at Goldentrees Residential Home could be significantly improved by an intake of *Jaffa Cakes*, let me tell you.

"Mrs. Osborne?" There's an inflection in her voice, she says my name as if she's asking me a question. Perhaps I should tell her that I'm not Mrs. Osborne, that I'm Myrtle Higginbotham. There's no point, the only victory I have is insisting the staff use my proper name. Some of the other residents like their Christian names being used. You should hear them, sounds like a roll call and I suppose it is. Harold, Jim, Elsie, Margaret. Sets my teeth on edge.

I'm Helen Osborne. I'm 82 and the only reason I'm here is

because I fell and broke my hip, and despite operations and hours and hours of physio, my hip is still not right. I'm not right.

I have a daughter, Kate, and she arranged it all. I couldn't do it. I'm still not sure if I should be here. Kate said, "Short of you moving in with us, Mum, this is the best solution and anyway, you'd never cope with our stairs."

Ha! Moving in with her, I knew that wouldn't work. Derek, her husband, he's older than Kate and I see the fear in his eyes. The fear of growing old: it's written all over him. He wouldn't want me living with them. Oh, he made all the right noises. "If it wasn't for the stairs, Helen, you know you'd be more than welcome. You know that." When people say things like "You know that," they're making sure you understand they're not being honest. All *I* knew was that Derek wanted me to think he was upset by the fact his house had three flights of stairs. He was delighted, job done, face saved.

Kate found Goldentrees and I sold my house for an eye-wateringly large sum of money, and here I am. This place is what my Mum would have called "posh". It's cushioned, that's what it feels like, cushioned against old age. The carpets in each bedroom are thick, expensive, and the curtains are lined and heavy. We eat well. "Cordon Bleu" is what the manager told Kate when she came to visit. Tiny portions of fish, glazed carrots and steamed vegetables. "All easy on the digestion," that's what the manager said. Might be easy but it's boring.

I talk to a few of the women here. They want to chat about their families, their health and how good the staff are. They also talk about the weather. I find that odd. Most of us are stuck here, and we can only look at what's going on in the outside world from behind the thick curtains. When we do go out, we're helped, someone supports us and we're eased into waiting cars, or sometimes taxis. The weather doesn't affect us any more, how can it? What does it matter if it rains, or if the sun is hot enough to fry your skull?

For the most part, their conversations run on easy lines and, as long as I don't wander away from those lines, we get on OK.

One of the things I've come to understand is that, as we age, people slip away from our lives. For a while, they're like barnacles: stuck to us as we wend our way through life. Then, one by one, they drop off. They die, they move, they simply drift away. Don't think I fully understood that until I put my house on the market and thought about telling people where I was going. There weren't that many people to tell. My neighbours wished me well, said the usual phrases: "Don't forget us, we'll come to see you." I went through my address book and sent off a few change of address cards. I wrote "Guess what? I'm moving into a residential home!" Why I put an exclamation mark after that, God knows. Anyway, the response was underwhelming. Thinking about it, I wondered if they thought I already lived in one? Who knows? It felt to me that, at the age of 82, the only people who matter to me are Kate and her two children, Amy and Thom. Can't count Derek, I just can't. My grandchildren have left home and live somewhere around the Sheffield area. They're twins, and when they left Sheffield Hallam University, they decided to stay nearby. I see the look on Kate's face when she talks of the distance between Bristol and Sheffield.

Amy and Thom send me texts, full of smiley faces and exclamation marks. All that energy, it makes me tired reading them. I often forget to charge my phone, so I don't always remember to reply. When I do remember, there doesn't seem to be a lot for me to tell them.

Oh, she's here, Kirsty with a cup of tea rattling in its saucer, two biscuits jammed alongside the cup.

"Do you want sugar, Mrs. Osborne?" Every day, *every* bloody day, she asks me that.

"No, thank you."

We stick to the niceties. All around me, I hear the noises from tea being slurped. The tea is tepid. It's 4.30 and I can't go to bed for hours.

In the morning, I hear the sound of the trolley again. It's like background music, a signature tune.

Today, Kate is coming. She's ordered me two nighties from M&S. She says if they're not right, she'll send them back. I miss shopping trips. A meander around the shops, a cup of tea and a slice of cake. Kate says no-one does that any longer, everything is online. Where's the fun in that?

She phoned last night, said she had something to tell me. She wouldn't say anything else. Maybe she's leaving Derek, maybe they're getting divorced. I read somewhere that children of divorced parents are more likely to split up. That's a guilt trip if ever there was one. She shouldn't have married Derek, but then I shouldn't have married her father. We divorced when Kate was about 12 or 13. Difficult to know who was more relieved, him or me. His name was Ralph. Kate tells me off when I say that. "He's not dead, Mum!" I prefer to think of him in the past tense. He moved away after we divorced, Scotland I think it was. Good riddance.

Someone said to me once that if I hadn't married him, I wouldn't have had Kate. What sort of a statement is that? Doesn't alter the fact that I loathed my ex-husband with every fibre of my being. I love Kate and I hated him.

It's odd and it might have something to do with sitting here, feeling suffocated by the Home, the residents and my inability to get away, but Ralph has crept into my mind. Like a burglar letting himself in through the back door, he's been walking around in my head, poking through my memories and dislodging my thoughts. I don't *want* to think about him, our marriage was toxic, a mistake and it made both of us unhappy. We got married because that's what our families wanted. My Mum and Dad knew Ralph's parents – simple as that. Their expectations carried us on a wave. It grew bigger and bigger and we went along with it. I've never been that passive since.

One memory keeps surfacing and it was when we arrived at our honeymoon destination: a week's holiday in Rome paid for by Ralph's parents. I can remember unpacking my case, putting my new clothes into the hotel wardrobe and once I'd closed the wardrobe door, I sat on the bed and wondered what I should do next. It felt to me as if I'd been on a voyage, everything was so organised, and once I'd arrived, there was nothing left to do. I know Ralph felt the same because I heard the tone in his voice when he asked, "What would you like to do now?" It was as if he was asking me what we *should* do, did I have a plan? I didn't.

I never went back to Rome, which is a shame, but it was permanently tainted for me. The city was always surrounded in the realisation that Ralph and I were married and neither of us knew what to do about it, about each other. Kate was conceived on our honeymoon. Never could rid myself of the feeling that Ralph thought he should, that it was something that was expected of him, part of his duties, being a groom to my bride. But then we had Kate and we made the best job we could of bringing her up. I'm proud of my daughter, very proud. She has her own company. She is a linguist and teaches French. She works for big companies as well as giving occasional lectures when she's asked. She's the main breadwinner as Derek took early retirement. He did something in electrical engineering. "Had enough of the rat race," he told me. *Rat race!* He hasn't got a clue. Now he spends most of his time in his allotment talking to the other men, nearly all of them hiding from their wives.

I worked; I was a teacher. I was good too. I taught English Literature. Ralph worked as an accountant, and after he left, I kept paying the mortgage and, to be fair, he paid maintenance for Kate. Every month, he never missed once. He'd come to see her, driving down from wherever he was living to spend time with her. All that politeness! All that smiling and stilted conversation. "How are you? I'm fine, how about you? Work going well?" As if on ice, our words skated over us, we were polite because of Kate who stood between us as she left me to spend time with her father. I ached when she walked away, her hand in Ralph's. She always turned to look at me and I smiled and waved, knowing my eyes were glassy with tears.

Before Kate came back from those outings, I paced the rooms of my house, checking my watch, wondering what she was doing, and how she was feeling. I knew she'd be safe with Ralph, of course I knew that, I just didn't want her to be with him. Every time she came back, I grabbed hold of her, reclaiming her and then I closed the door before Ralph had turned to leave.

Kate and I survived that, and her father became a topic we never discussed. When birthday and Christmas cards arrived for her, she took them upstairs to her bedroom to put them on display on her shelves. I didn't question that, as it was her business not mine.

She saw him throughout her time at university and I know he's been to her house and I know he's a fond grandfather to the twins because sometimes Kate will drop him into the conversation, "Dad went to see the kids last week. Took them out to lunch apparently."

"That's nice." We talked like that, Kate mentioning her Dad and me acknowledging the fact.

She said to me that he'd moved, somewhere near Birmingham. "Found a bungalow near a park, got a lake he said."

"Sounds nice."

"He told me he's struggling a bit with stairs so that's why he moved."

"Oh, is he?"

Ralph was, *is*, a year older than me.

She hadn't mentioned him for a while and I was all right with that.

The morning passed. To be fair, the staff do their best to keep us all occupied or amused. They don't think we can do both, but someone came. It may have been Mandy, or was it Cindy? She turns up once a week for armchair aerobics. The music is so loud that if anyone asked a question, she'd never hear it. Mandy or Cindy, or whatever her name is, is always telling me I should take part. "It'd do you the world of good, keeps your muscles in shape." She makes them sound like knicker elastic. I don't go, I don't see the point.

There's a hairdresser too, she comes once a week, but Kate knows I don't like the way she does my hair, so when she can, Kate takes me to her hairdressers. I much prefer that. For a while, I feel back in the world again where I can sit and drink tea and gossip and pretend that, instead of going back to Goldentrees, I can leave the salon and go home, to my home. It's silly I know, but I even like the smell of the salon, the shampoo, the conditioner. They smell different and that smell stays with me. It makes me feel special.

I read my book, it's quite good and then it was lunchtime. It was a Tuesday, so it was ham salad. There was excitement a few weeks ago when Molly Evans swore blind that she'd seen a caterpillar in her lettuce. She was wrong, but for a few days, everyone talked about the times they'd found things in their meals. You should have heard them; there were tales of slugs, of finger nails, of long hairs in bowls of soup. They all tried to outdo each other in terms of outrage. "I told the waiter I wasn't paying good money to have hairs in my soup."

For a while, I heard the satisfaction in their voices: they might be living in a Home, their glory days might be behind them, but when they were younger, they'd been forces to be reckoned with, they'd never taken things lying down.

Must have been Kirsty's day off because another woman brought me my lunch. I like her, she smiles a lot. She makes me feel as if she's pleased to see me. "Mrs. Osborne! Look at you today! Such a nice colour you're wearing."

She might say that to all the residents, I don't know and I don't care. Her name is Rosie and I can hear her humming as she walks up and down the corridors. Far better sound than the one I hear from Kirsty's *Crocs*.

I ate my lunch while looking out of the window at the lawns and the gardens. The sun was shining and the trees were moving. It was October and the leaves were dropping. I like Autumn best of all. Spring I always felt was too loud, all that bursting forth and new buds to cope with, and Summer, well I can still remember trying to work out what Kate and I could do every day to eke out the time before she and I went back to school. I didn't teach at Kate's school. I wouldn't have inflicted that on her. Autumn was a new term, there'd be new children to teach, the smell of new shoes and the fading of the trees with the wonderful colours to enjoy. Winter, no, never could get on with winter. It was always so cold and dark. No, Autumn is the best season.

Rosie came to take my tray away and she brought me a cup of tea. I thanked her and told her that my daughter was coming to see me. "Would you bring her a cup of tea too?"

Rosie nodded, "Of course I will. It'll be nice for you to see your daughter."

Nice. Such a bland word, but I knew what Rosie meant. Kate is my only visitor and therefore it will be nice to see her.

I must have dozed off which irritated me as I hoped I hadn't been sleeping with my mouth open. That's not an image I'm comfortable with. Anyway, Kate touched my shoulder, "Mum, hello, wake up."

"Oh," I shook my head trying to dislodge the sleepiness. "Must have closed my eyes for a second." Neither of us believed me.

"Here, Mum, I've brought you the nighties. They look a bit big to me, you've lost some weight, but if they don't fit, I can send them back."

She put the package in my lap and I touched the plastic covering. I didn't want to waste the time I had with Kate by trying on nighties, so I told her I'd do it later and she put the package onto the bed.

She sat down opposite me and immediately touched my hand. "Mum, listen to me, there's something I want to tell you."

"Oh, good God, whatever is it? You look as if someone has died." I put a hand to my throat, "Oh, Kate, it's not the twins is it? Tell me they're all right."

She shook her head and her voice was tetchy, "*No*, it's nothing to do with the twins although neither of them seem capable of letting me know they're OK but," she shrugged, "if anything happened to them, I'd know soon enough. They're fine."

"Then what is it? You look so serious."

Kate stroked the base of my thumb, "It's Dad."

"Oh, so *he's* died?"

"*No!* Mum, for God's sake, no-one's died. Just listen to me."

I didn't like the tone of Kate's voice, but I kept quiet and I watched her fingers stroke my thumb as if by stroking me, she was keeping me calm.

She took a deep breath, "Dad will be moving in here, here at Goldentrees."

I jerked back as if I'd been shot. "*What?* No, that can't be right. He's living in a bungalow near, where was it, *Bournemouth*? You told me that! You've got it wrong. Not *here*, he can't come here. You've made a mistake."

She closed her eyes, her voice was breathy, low. "He is coming here, Mum. He's coming next week." She took a deep breath, "Will you listen to me?"

I felt her pressure on my hand and I tried to pull away, but she tightened her grip and wouldn't let go.

I shook my head, "No, I'm not listening. I'm not. I don't want him here."

"Mum, please, this is hard enough for me. He is coming here because I can't keep track of both of you. You here and Dad up the M5, the kids in bloody Sheffield and I'm trying to keep everything ticking over." She sat back, her grip on my hand eased and I yanked it away from her.

I glared at her, "In that case, *I'll* leave here. I'll find somewhere else. I'll go home…"

Kate shook her head, "Mum, this is your home and you can't leave here because there is nowhere else. God *knows* I tried hard to find somewhere you'd like." She lifted her head, "Mum, you're not, well, truth is you're not easy at the best of times and this really is the best place for you."

I wrapped my arms across my chest, "In that case tell *him*, your father, that he'll have to find somewhere else."

"No, I won't. "She looked at me, "Have you *any* idea how hard it's been for me? I'm working full-time, trying to keep my eye on you and Dad, in two different parts of the country, two kids who think it's OK to ring home whenever they need something, usually money and Derek who…" she shook her head. "I'm not Wonder Woman, Mum. I'm just me." She looked at me, her gaze was steady. "I've had to cope with a lot, Mum, over the years."

There it was. The whole parcel of stuff we never talk about. Her Dad, my ex-husband. Now I come to think about it, it was a bit like a parcel. Kate trying to pass it to me over the years, and me never wanting to take delivery. I sat back, I felt winded.

"Oh."

Kate stood and walked over to the window. She looked out and her voice was muffled. "For all my life, I've had to keep my parents apart. Not just physically, although I suspect that was the easiest part, but always being careful not to mention you to Dad or him to you. The obvious way to describe it is that it was like walking through a minefield, but oh God, it was worse than that! I didn't want to go *into* the field, never mind keeping away from the mines!" Her voice had risen and I kept quiet.

She turned and her eyes were wet, "You're both in your eighties, you're both as stubborn as mules and you both need help and there's just me to give it."

"Kate…"

She lifted a hand, "No, I haven't finished. For *years*, Mum, I've tried to be a good daughter to you both and it was like being in a parallel universe. You occupy two different parts of my life: a compartment for you and another one for Dad. Have you any idea how bloody hard it's been?"

She moved again and grabbed the back of a chair and I watched her take a deep breath. I felt my heart rate increase, but I couldn't take my eyes off Kate's face.

"You're a force to be reckoned with, Mum and I know you don't like it here, because the staff tell me how awkward you've made things for them. They don't use the words *difficult* or *rude*, they're my words because I know you, I know you very well."

I looked at my lap, at my hands, devoid of any jewellery. My mouth was dry, but I didn't think a cup of tea would help.

Kate looked at me, "Whether you like it or not, Dad *will* be moving in here because I'm his daughter as well as yours and this is the best way for me to keep an eye on you both. There is no other option, Mum, believe me I've tried. Not just for your sake, but for mine and Dad's and actually because of the staff here. They're good people, all of them, working hard to keep you safe and that's what I need to know, that you're both being looked after."

I heard the *whoosh* as she breathed out.

Her voice when she spoke was low, "Mum, I'm so sick of juggling everything all the time. I'm bloody sick of it."

I shifted in my chair, trying to move away from Kate's anger and distress. "I'm sorry about that."

"*Are* you?"

I flinched, her question was direct, her gaze harsh. "Yes, of course I am."

Kate moved around my room as if she she'd been sitting still for too long and she wanted to stretch her legs. "All my life, Mum, I've been forced to keep the pair of you apart. I've got friends whose parents have divorced and they grumble about trying to juggle stuff, trying not to upset one parent because they're trying to please the other one." She stopped her pacing, "At least my friends' parents understood that, even recognised it. But you, dear God, you're in a league of your own. You flatly refused to acknowledge that Dad even *existed*!"

I waved my arm around, trying to shoo her words away, "I did my best for you."

"Did you?"

I nodded, my voice was a whisper, "I did, you know I did."

Kate looked at me, "Did you know, for a long time I used to tell my friends that Dad had died?"

I shook my head, "Lots of kids do that when their parents get divorced."

"No they don't!" She took a breath, "What you've done, even more than Dad, is make me feel as if I can't tell you anything…"

"No, no, that's not fair! That's not fair at all. I always encouraged you to talk to me, to tell me what you were feeling, what was upsetting you."

Kate laughed, her laugh was harsh, "Yeah, you did that all right, but I could never talk to you about Dad, could I? And now, guess what, that legacy of not telling you about Dad has somehow leaked into my marriage, my …oh, what's the point?"

I kept quiet and watched my daughter, I watched the expressions chase across her face and, for the first time, I realised Kate was growing older. I frowned, she must be, what? Coming up to fifty. Was she? Was she *really* that old?

I cleared my throat, "Kate, what's wrong with your marriage?"

She glanced at me, almost as if she'd forgotten I was there. She sighed, "D'you know, Mum, I watched an old programme the other night, one about variety shows and I saw a man, a juggler and he ran around the stage trying to keep plates balancing on poles. Seemed a stupid waste of time to me, and then I recognised it took skill, but I wondered why he was doing it. All that effort." She pulled a face, "That's what I've been doing, *plate juggling*, and Derek, well, let's say Derek wouldn't care if they all fell to the floor and smashed."

I felt such sadness as I realised that Kate had said more to me in the last ten minutes, *real* conversation, than she'd said in, well, a long time. And her marriage, was that in trouble? I understood that I couldn't say much, do much, because of my behaviour and my attitude towards Derek. My own disastrous marriage had clouded my vision of my daughter's marriage. I'd viewed all men, all husbands, as useless. Maybe Derek *was* useless, but he wasn't my problem. Either way, I hated to see the distress on Kate and to know I'd played a big part in that distress.

She was still pacing up and down the room, occasionally looking at me, occasionally looking out of the window.

"Kate, please sit down. Please." I kept my voice low, wanting to comfort her.

For a moment, I thought she'd refuse, but then with a sigh, she sat and faced me.

"I'm sorry," I pulled a face, "All I was concentrating on was my own anger at the way my marriage had turned out. And, to be honest, I went into marriage as if I was on automatic pilot and *that* I'd always regretted." Kate shifted and I spoke quickly, "I bitterly regret the hurt I've caused you and I can't make up for all those years, but from now, I'll try harder, I promise I will." I meant that promise knowing that nothing I said could ever wipe out what I'd done, but maybe I could stop myself from hurting her in the future.

"Mum," Kate frowned, "What about, Dad? Will you at least try to get on with him?"

I didn't know how to answer that, so I told her that out of the blue, I'd been thinking about him. "Maybe I had a premonition." I smiled and Kate's smile was brief. We both knew my words meant nothing more than an attempt at easing a difficult conversation.

Just then Rosie knocked on the door and I felt some of the tension leave the room.

"Hello," Rosie's smile was broad, "Cups of tea for you both?" The trolley was at her side and Kate rose immediately to help her bring it into my room.

Rosie chattered on about something on TV the night before and

Kate said she'd seen it too and they both tried to include me in their conversation, but I hadn't watched the programme. I knew I'd been an outsider for most of my life, not wanting to become part of much and, without either of them noticing, I felt distressed, tearful. What had I done?

Rosie handed me a cup of tea, with the *Rich Tea* biscuits slotted, as always, in the saucer

Kate took her cup and then we watched Rosie wheel the trolley out of the room.

"Bye, Mrs. Osborne," Rosie smiled, "I'll see you later."

The silence after she'd gone was heavy, filling the room, and neither Kate nor I spoke. We drank the tea and nibbled on the biscuits. I thought they were on the stale side.

I didn't know what to do, what to say to make things right and, not sure what prompted it other than a need to let Kate know that I would change my behaviour, be more receptive, I blurted out, "I'll tell the staff to call me Helen."

She smiled, "That's good, Mum."

Neither of us mentioned her Dad again, but when Kate left, we both knew that, when he arrived, even though I wouldn't welcome him with open arms, at least I'd let him know about the life in Goldentrees. I'd tell him that's it's not all bad, that the staff are kind and caring, and maybe he might enjoy the *Rich Tea* biscuits. I wouldn't know that about him, but then he wouldn't know that I prefer *Jaffa Cakes*.

An Act of Quiet Rebellion

Ellie's gifts were always beautifully wrapped. This one had golden paper topped with a glittering bow. She handed it over, her smile bright. "Just a little something for your birthday. I hope it makes you smile."

I always thanked her and always felt a knot of apprehension because her gifts were extravagant and, this time, on my birthday, when I opened the gift, I found seven pairs of socks. They weren't the sort of socks to be found in a chain store, not these. These socks had been made from what? I frowned, cashmere? They were beautifully soft and, as I held them up, I saw that each day of the week had been embroidered across each instep. There they were: Monday through to Sunday. Why did socks with the days of the week depress me?

See, the thing is, Ellie is, how can I put this? She's not like me, not in any way. I'm a bit slapdash, a bit of an "Oh, it will do," sort of person. I get things done, well, nearly always. Ellie has to be the most organised person on the planet. For example, each night, Ellie lays out her clothes for the following day. She told me that she did this in case there were any nasty surprises. I had no idea what she meant and she said, one eyebrow slightly raised, "A mark on a blouse, or a broken zip."

I don't know if that's impressive or scary. Either way, I don't want to do that. I can't do that. I've got two teenage daughters and whatever I think about putting on in the morning, either I can't find it because one of the girls has borrowed it, or the other one has worn it and it's sitting in the laundry basket. I work too, admittedly from home, and sometimes, I need to look presentable. I'm an editor at a publishing house for children's books and there are days when I'm meeting an author or have a Zoom conference. I cheat a bit on those days. The top half looks OK, but the bottom half, well, I favour comfort over image. I laughed when I said that to Ellie and she shook her head, "I couldn't do that. It would make me uneasy. I need to look the best I can."

I met Ellie by chance. Working from home is great, but at times I need to clear my head, to get fresh air and I've been in the habit of taking an hour's walk first thing in the morning. I wear tracksuit bottoms, a baggy tee-shirt, maybe a hoodie and I listen to music as I walk. I find that walk energising and once I've showered, I can start my day.

It was about eighteen months ago when I came across Ellie. She was holding on to a lead and, at the end of the lead, was an energetic labradoodle. All fur and no sense of direction. I laughed because the dog had somehow wrapped the lead around Ellie's legs and sat looking up at her, expecting her to sort it out. "Here, let me help." Between us, we got her free.

Holding out her hand, Ellie introduced herself and we walked to the end of the path and turned and came back. She told me that the dog wasn't hers, she was walking it for a friend "And I won't be doing this again." She showed me one tracksuited leg and I could see splodges of mud where the dog had jumped up at her. She said she'd not long moved into the house near the fields. She told me that she was divorced, she had no children and she worked for a bank. She also worked from home for three days of the week and, somehow, never sure how, we fell into a routine of walking when we were both free.

I liked her, still do, but I was always aware that Ellie's life, her home and her job were wildly different from mine. That's not a bad thing, of course it's not, but I vividly remember seeing inside Ellie's house for the first time. I'd knocked on her door one morning, I'd been early and she invited me in. Seeing how she lived made me understand how different we were. If I say that Ellie's kitchen could have been used for open heart surgery, you'll know what I mean. Nothing was out of place and that was because there was nothing in the kitchen. There was no kettle, no mug rack, no toaster, not even a jar of instant coffee. Oh, that's not totally true. A pot of basil was on the windowsill and a dark green tea-towel hung near the oven. Everything was colour coordinated. That was it. Seriously, that was it. I had to close my eyes for a second because, no matter how hard I tried, I couldn't dislodge the image of *my* kitchen and how I'd left it that morning. There was the usual assortment of dishes piled in the sink. My girls are clever, but neither of them has grasped the fact that dirty dishes can be put into the dishwasher. The bread we'd used for toast was on the table next to a tray of minced beef I'd taken from the freezer to make a pot of chilli for supper. A jumbled collection of cardigans and sweaters was draped over the backs of the chairs and the newspaper my husband, Phil, had been reading, was in a heap near the fridge. He'd grumbled that he couldn't finish the crossword, telling me he'd try it again when he came home. Was my kitchen scruffy? Maybe, but that was how my family operated, how *I* operated. What's the phrase? I don't sweat the small stuff.

So, looking at Ellie's kitchen with its pristine work surfaces, gleaming taps and shiny floor, depressed and in a peculiar way, intimidated me. I wondered if I should rush home and blitz my kitchen, my home. I didn't. I had far too much work to do, so when I got home, I closed the kitchen door. I'd sort it out, later.

Not sure why, but in a peculiar, masochistic way, I enjoyed her company. We walked and put the world to rights, chatting about various things as women do: whether I should change my hair colour, whether Ellie needed a new handbag for the summer. They were superficial things, but we also talked about bigger issues: politics, global warming and books. We talked a lot about books. Ellie was an avid reader and we often had a book club type discussion. I enjoyed those the most. We both loved Elizabeth Strout's novels and couldn't understand why anyone would read anything by Dan Brown.

One day, she asked if I'd like to have a cup of coffee with her after we'd walked. Truth was, I didn't really have the time. I had a deadline, yet there was something in her voice, not sure how to describe it, but I sensed wistfulness. Anyway, I said "yes".

We sat in her living room and, if her kitchen was immaculate, her living room resembled a show home. You've seen them, lavishly presented houses where builders try to convince you that you too can have a house, a *life*, just like the one they're trying to sell. Ellie had told me that she liked neutral colours and her room was pale biscuit. Pale biscuit *everywhere*. It was like sitting in a bowl of porridge. The walls held four prints, subdued colours of different areas of Italy. Three silver-framed photos were on the mantelpiece, and one pot plant with impossibly glossy leaves. I couldn't take my eyes away from that plant. She must have polished the leaves. She must have done. Who does that?

I was uneasy, uncomfortable, so I sat, perched on the edge of her cream sofa holding a cup and saucer in my nervous hand. Cup and saucer! I tried to listen to Ellie talking about her boss, how difficult he was, but all I could think about was whether I had matching cups and saucers, because, of course, I'd have to invite Ellie to my home too.

Phil was bemused. "What on *earth* are you doing? She's a neighbour, not the Queen."

"I know, I know," I snapped. "It's just that sometimes our house looks like a tornado has gone right through it."

Phil grinned, "Yeah, we have two of those: our daughters."

"You're not helping."

Why was I so anxious? Why did I *care* what Ellie might think about my home? I knew the answer to that, and it's not something I wanted to think about, so I pushed it away.

Phil tried to be helpful, putting books back on the shelves, lining up the magazines on the coffee table. He removed the collection of mugs and plates littering the surfaces in the kitchen and between us, our home looked, if not *Homes and Gardens*, then less like a squat.

Phil touched my shoulder, "Sweetheart, this is our home where four people live. It's lived in. That's a good thing."

Yeah, maybe. I still worried what Ellie would make of my home. And me. There's something about opening up your home to other people that's frightening. It's a form of exposure and I knew what I'd thought about Ellie's pristine home, what that suggested to me about her, about the life she lived, about her solitariness. Yet here I was, doing the same thing, opening up my home for her to judge me. Phil said she wouldn't do that, but what does he know?

"This is nice," she said, her eyes taking in the scuff marks on the skirting boards and the curtains that had never hung properly. Why hadn't I done anything about those? She sat, just like I had in her house: perched on the edge of a chair. I'd found china mugs and was pleased that I could also offer her fresh coffee. I remembered reading somewhere that estate agents say that the smell of fresh coffee always impresses prospective buyers. Got no idea why that had come into my head.

Ellie sipped at her coffee, telling me that the bank was in the process of streamlining the workforce and, whilst she thought she would be OK in the long term, it meant that she would be working from home all the time. "I thought," she smiled at me, "maybe we could take longer walks or perhaps think about going out for a coffee, or lunch or something."

I smiled, "That sounds good, but my hours are a bit erratic at the best of times..." I didn't know what else to say. Part of me wanted to say that, whilst her working life might be stabilising, mine wasn't. That wasn't all I wanted to say because I wasn't sure exactly what I was feeling. I concentrated on sipping at the strong coffee I'd made.

After that, Ellie came up with all sorts of suggestions: "Maybe we could walk an hour earlier tomorrow. We'll get more out of the day. Hope you don't mind me saying this, but you really should think about buying better quality trainers. Couldn't help but notice how old yours are. See, if you're serious about walking and we will be doing more, then you should invest in a better pair. It's false economy..." I blotted out the rest.

Somehow, and although it sounds odd, my walking changed shape. Where once it had been enjoyable, freeing, calming, where I could listen to *Fleetwood Mac* on my headphones or listen to the birdsong, it had now become an obstacle course. It got serious, organised and I didn't like it, not one bit. Ellie appeared to be on a mission, to improve me, to re-educate me, to *smarten* me. I started obsessing about what I should wear when I walked, worrying about the state of my T-shirts, my jogging trousers.

When I grumbled to Phil, he did what most men do, said I was making too much of it. "Just tell her you don't want to walk with her any longer. It doesn't need to be complicated."

I couldn't say that to her. At least, I didn't think I could, not without hurting her, and it was complicated.

The first time Ellie bought me a present, it had been my birthday and her gift had been thoughtful: a gold-coloured cafetiere with a pack of expensive coffee. "I thought you'd like this on your desk, when you work."

I thanked her and ignored Phil's expression. I also ignored his comment about needing to clear a space for it.

For her birthday, I found a quirky print of a seaside town she said she'd visited as a child. I thought it was a real find: scarlet frame and vibrant colours of the cottages overlooking the bay. She said she liked it, but I never saw it again.

Ellie's gifts were expensive, tasteful and I pushed away the feeling that she was still trying to change me, make me sophisticated. Once I told her how, years ago, the girls had gone to school with Sellotape on the hems of their school skirts. "I repaired them properly when they came home." I spoke rapidly, registering Ellie's look of disapproval. "I didn't have time." I'd stopped. Why did I say these things to her and then feel the need to defend myself?

To be honest, there were times when I thought about not walking, or going somewhere different, even driving to another area, just so I could walk on my own. I struggled with that, knowing how much Ellie enjoyed our walks. She'd told me that many times. I found the whole thing confusing and my thought processes were wandering all over the place. What did I represent to Ellie and her to me? My ying to her yang? Don't even know if I got that right.

Then Ellie presented me with the socks. She'd smiled when she saw me looking at a day of the week beautifully embroidered on each pair. "That way," she touched my arm, "you'll know where you are in the week."

When I showed them to Phil, he whistled in appreciation. "Wow, they make a change from the ones you normally wear."

And they did. Their colours were wonderful: muted shades of cream, grey and soft rose pink. They were gorgeous. I put them in the drawer alongside my grey socks, the ones that had once been black, the ones where the heels were rubbed and the fabric resembled a sieve. I shut the drawer, not wanting to look at them, not really understanding my rush to put them out of sight.

When I next met Ellie, she was wearing a pair of dark blue leggings, her hoodie was clean and her trainers looked as if she'd just taken them out of a box. I'd made an effort too. I was wearing a pair of the socks that Ellie had given to me. My tracksuit bottom was old but clean, my T-shirt, with a faded *Duran Duran* logo, had once belonged to Phil and my trainers were my usual pair: soft, worn, comfortable. I had put new laces in though. I saw the way Ellie looked at my trainers and decided to ignore the expression on her face.

Determined not to let her intimidate me in any way and to make her understand that I was making an effort, I said, "I'm wearing the socks you gave me."

"Oh, are you?" Her tone was full of meaning. "I'm glad you like them."

"I do." I kept the smile, didn't waver once.

Ellie's smile was smug and I didn't tell her, but on my left foot, I wore a sock with *Thursday* written on it and on the right foot, the sock said *Saturday*.

"Shall we go?" I touched Ellie's hand as we crossed the road. I could do this, of course I could. All I needed was an act of quiet rebellion.

Trolley Boss

All the kids call me Bernie. I don't mind. My Mum says every one of my names: Bernard James Robert Phillips and then she asks me a question, "What am I going to do with you?" When she says that she doesn't say it with a cross face, she sort of sings my name and she gives me a hug when she comes to Phillips. I think it's because she's got the same name as me, Phillips.

She gets very tired, my Mum. She says things like, "Bernard James Robert Phillips, you'll be the death of me." I don't like it when she says that. I know about death from when my Dad and Uncle George died. That was death. Mum explained it to me, about why they'd died and how they'd both gone to heaven. She said it was a place full of angels, and now Dad and Uncle George are up there too and their white wings flutter and, at Christmas, some of their tiny feathers fall and that makes the snow.

I like Christmas. That's when Mum and I go to the big church in town and I sing all the carols. *Away in the Manger* is my favourite. I can't always remember the words, but Mum says to do my best and just hum if I'm not sure. People look at me when I hum though. Mum says to ignore them, but they keep staring.

Last Christmas, I bought Mum a box of *Quality Street*. Auntie Betty said it was the biggest box she'd ever seen. She said she'd have to help Mum eat them all. Auntie Betty also chose a scarf for me to give to Mum as well. She said I could pay her back later, but I forgot.

I earn £20 a week. And it's all mine. I can keep every penny. Mum said I could. She found my job for me. It's at the supermarket where she goes every Friday. She kept saying it was a disgrace that there were never any trolleys around when people needed them. She said it was criminal the way people left them hanging about in the car park. "Why can't people take them back for others to use them?" She was always going on about it.

She told the manager, Mr. Abrahams, all about me. She didn't say anything to me about getting a job, but she knew I wanted one. She just came home from the supermarket one Friday and said that she'd had a word with the manager. "I told him that you're trustworthy and reliable. You won't let me down, will you, Bernard?"

She held my hands when she was telling me about the job. She kept staring at me. "Now listen to me, Bernard. The manager is a very kind man, but he's a very busy man too. He doesn't have the time to check up on what you're doing. It will be your job to bring all the trolleys back from the car park and take them to the area near the door. That's what you do, that's all you do. Do you understand me? Are you listening to me?"

She wouldn't let go of my hands until I promised I'd do exactly as I was told.

"This is important, Bernard, promise me."

I didn't like the way she was staring at me. Her eyes didn't blink once. I felt funny when she did that and I tried to move my head away. Mum let go of my hands then and grabbed the sides of my head.

"Look at me, Bernard." She was using her stern voice. I didn't like it. She was making me nervous. I wriggled and tried to pull her hands away, but she can be really strong sometimes and, so in the end, I had to look at her.

"You must promise me, Bernard, that you'll do everything

71

you're told. Do you promise me?"

I promised, I gave her my word of honour. I even did my special salute. I can still remember it from when I was in the Scouts.

She laughed and gave me a hug. "OK, Bernard James Robert Phillips – how about tea and biscuits to dunk?"

Before I started work, I had to meet the manager, Mr. Abrahams. Mum took me on a Wednesday morning. She made me put on a clean shirt and she said she didn't think it was a good idea to wear my baseball cap. Mr. Abrahams kept us waiting for ages. We went there on time, 11 o'clock, but even when it was almost 12 o'clock, we were still waiting outside his office.

"Why doesn't he come? We always have our soup at 12 o'clock. Did you tell him that, Mum?"

Mum didn't answer me, she just shook her head and whispered that I mustn't be too loud.

When Mr. Abrahams came out of his office, I put my hand out to shake his. Perhaps he didn't notice because he shook Mum's hand, not mine. But he did ask me to sit down when we were in his office.

He asked Mum loads of questions about me: was I strong, could I manage on my own and then he asked, "Does he need help with getting to the toilet…or anything?"

He looked at me when he said "toilet" and I wanted to say something to him, to let him know that I wasn't a baby, I could manage. I could go to the toilet on my own, but Mum put her hand out and held mine. That's her signal, we worked it out ages ago, and it means that I must keep quiet. "Even if people say something that upsets you or hurts you, don't let them see that, just smile."

So I did. I smiled at Mr. Abrahams, but even then he wasn't looking at me, he was looking at Mum.

"Bernard can cope perfectly well on his own, he won't need any help at all." Mum sat up straight as she spoke and she wasn't smiling then. Mr. Abrahams looked at me, but it was a really quick look, so I don't think he noticed me smiling at him.

"You understand, Mrs. Phillips, that neither I nor my staff have got time to spare for, well, for helping Bernard. He'll have to manage on his own."

He hadn't heard Mum, hadn't heard her say that I could manage all by myself. I tried to move, I wanted to tell him again, but Mum's hands were holding mine and she was holding on tight, she was hurting me and I knew she wanted me to sit still and not say a word, so I didn't.

Then Mum tugged at my arm when Mr. Abrahams stood up and we both stood as he opened the door of his office.

Mum sighed, she does that sometimes when people have upset her and she held my hand again when we were outside the office. "Do you understand, Bernard? Do you know what you've got to do? It's a few hours a day collecting the trolleys. Do you think you can manage that?"

I nodded at her and she laughed and said that if I nodded any harder my head would fall off. I laughed too and we walked out of the supermarket. Mum told me to stand still and wait for her by the door and she went back in again. When she came out, she was holding two Mars bars.

"One for you, Bernard James Robert Phillips, and one for me."

I told her I'd keep mine for later or I wouldn't eat my lunch. She gave me a hug and said I'd be the death of her.

I was so excited the night before I started my job. Mum said I was even worse than the night before my birthday. My birthday's in May. Each year, she says I must learn to act like an adult. Every time my birthday comes, she says it and I'm forty-three now. Mum says I'm like a bull, charging around after things. She says she didn't believe all that nonsense about star signs, before I was born, but she does now.

She bought me a new pair of trousers when I started working at the supermarket. "I want you to look smart, you're doing an important job. You're in charge of the trolleys. Mr. Abrahams is your boss, but you're the boss of all those trolleys."

I know a lot of the people who shop at the supermarket: there's Mr. and Mrs. Cummings, they live near the library and there's Mrs. Armstrong, she works in the Post Office and that woman Mum doesn't like, the one with the twins, Julie and Kate. Everyone knows about my job and they tell me what a difference I'm making. "A pleasure to do my shopping now," Mrs. Cummings said that to me. When I told Mum what she'd said, Mum had tears in her eyes. She said she didn't, but I could see them.

It's hard work, my job. There's a lot of standing and watching. Some people just push their trolleys away after they've finished with them. They send them into the sides of other cars so that's why I watch. Sometimes I walk behind people as they leave the supermarket and I watch them to see they don't just leave them or push them against cars. They mustn't do that and it's my job to see that the trolleys aren't damaged. People think that trolleys aren't important, but they are. I'm in charge of them, I'm their boss.

I took my pay envelope home to show Mum. The big, fat girl who works in the office came out to the car park. She gave me the envelope, it had my name on it: Bernard Phillips. I told her that I had other names as well. "Bernard James Robert Phillips." I told her that, but she wasn't listening. She kept looking over her shoulder all the time, some of the other girls in the supermarket were watching her.

Mum asked why I hadn't opened my envelope. "It's got your name on it, you've earned it." She said she'd put the money in the Post Office for me and she gave me a hug. "I'm so proud of you, Bernard. You're doing a very good job."

I liked my job, being in charge of the trolleys. I didn't like it when people left plastic bags in them or bits of orange peel or crisps packets. They shouldn't do that, it's not nice. I got some carrier bags from the supermarket and put all the rubbish in them. Mr. Abrahams came out once to see me. He saw me putting rubbish in the bags and he said I was doing a good job. He gave me a badge too, it had my name on it: *Bernard* written in red letters. He said I should wear it on my jumper. I told him about my other names, but he shook his head.

"I don't think the badge is big enough for all that, Bernard." He was in a hurry. Mum keeps telling me that he's a busy man.

"Everything all right, Bernard? Got any problems?" He'd started to walk away without waiting for me to answer him.

"No, no problems, I can manage. I like looking after the trolleys."

I wanted him to know that. I wanted him to look at my trolleys, see how clean they were, see how I kept them parked in the proper place.

But Mr. Abrahams just walked off, he only said, "Good, that's good." And he didn't look at the trolleys.

Some lads started to come into the car park. At first it was all right, they gave me crisps and chocolate. Some of them smoked. I told them it was a bad thing, as you can get cancer, but they laughed at me. They said they didn't care, they said I shouldn't let things like that worry me.

They came every day, even when they should have been in school. They brought big bottles of cider and when they'd drunk it, they left the empty bottles in the trolley. They pushed the trolleys up and down the car park, they even started riding in them and shouting at other people. I told them not to do it, I said I was in charge of the trolleys and they were making a mess of them. I didn't like it.

One of them, the one called Carl, tried to pull my badge off my jumper. I said it was mine, I said Mr. Abrahams had given it to me for being in charge of the trolleys.

Carl asked me why my name was Bernard. "Did your mother call you that after one of those big, slobbering dogs?"

I didn't know what he meant. "No, I'm called Bernard after my Dad. He died, he's in heaven now."

"Yeah, bet he is, must have been the shock after seeing you..."

Carl and his friends came in every day. They'd come in all the time and I didn't know what to do. I told Mum and she said that I was only there to tidy up the trolleys, nothing else. "Just do what you're paid to do, Bernard. Don't get involved."

Carl and his gang were in the car park again last week. There were a lot of them and they'd been drinking. They dropped cans of beer and bottles of cider everywhere. One of them had been sick, it was all over the seat of one of the trolleys. I told Carl that they mustn't do that, it was my job to take care of the trolleys. He said, "Fuck off, moron."

I pushed the trolleys back to the right place. I got a cloth to clean the sick up. Carl and his gang walked behind me and they were all laughing. I told them it wasn't funny, I told them that they mustn't come to the car park again if they wouldn't look after the trolleys. They laughed and called me names: *Barmy Bernard,*

Bollocks Bernard, Bernard's a bugger.

They wouldn't stop, they shouted at me all the time. *Barmy Bernard, Barmy Bernard.*

Everyone was looking at me, girls from the supermarket were pointing, staring out through the big windows. Then Mr. Abrahams came out, he was walking really fast. Carl and his gang ran away when they saw him.

"Bernard? What's going on? Are you all right? Did they hurt you?" Mr. Abrahams' face was all red and his hair was sticking up.

I told him I was OK, I told him that I'd clean up the trolleys. I said it wasn't my fault, I said I didn't make the mess. "I look after the trolleys. I'm in charge of them."

"Yes, OK, that's OK." He walked back to the supermarket and I saw him talking to one of the girls by the door. They stood there looking at me. I thought they were cross about the mess in the trolleys. I cleaned it all up, every bit of sick. But it wasn't my fault.

Mr. Abrahams phoned Mum last night. She was in our hall and all I could hear her say was, "But that's not fair, it wasn't his fault, that's not fair…"

When she finished talking to Mr. Abrahams, Mum came back into the living room. She had two red patches on her cheeks. She sat down on the couch next to me and held my hands.

"Listen to me, Bernard. You can't go to the supermarket anymore. Mr. Abrahams says he doesn't want any trouble. He knows it's not your fault, but he says you can't look after the trolleys any longer. Do you understand?"

"No! I did a good job. I didn't make the mess, those boys did! I'm in charge of the trolleys. It wasn't me! That's not fair."

Mum was holding my hands very tight. "I know, son. I'm sorry."

I went to the supermarket this morning. There were two big blokes there, they were just standing around, smoking. They were wearing blue jumpers, although they didn't have name badges. The word *Security* was on the back of their jumpers. I didn't go into the car park. I only stood near the trolley park.

One of the blokes told me to move away and I shook my head. Then the other one said, "Piss off, you're scaring the customers."

I'm not. I wouldn't do that. I only want to watch to see that people put the trolleys away properly. I've still got my badge, Mum said she didn't think Mr. Abrahams would mind if I kept it. I will, even though it hasn't got all my names on it. Mum said everyone who knows me, knows my name is Bernard.

Some Sort of Twilight

I'd printed it all off. There were four sheets of paper, all of them on the table on top of the mail that Mum had brought in yesterday. She always picks the mail up from the mat when she gets home. She says she's got to be in the right mood to open mail, so it's often left there for a few days. She says she's got enough to worry about, getting to work on time, without having to think about what's in the post. The thing is, there's very little in the post these days, just circulars, flyers from Domino's Pizza and, for some reason, she keeps getting letters from a company specialising in retirement homes. "Bloody cheek," she said the first time she'd seen it.

She hasn't seen the sheets of paper, not yet. I thought about shoving them in the middle of the pile of post, sort of hiding them from view, but then I thought that was stupid. So there they are, next to the salt and pepper pots Mum had brought back from a day trip she took with her mates from work. They went to Porthcawl, sixteen of them on a coach. She said the salt and pepper pots reminded her of me when I was a baby, two fat-faced cherubs, one with Salt, the other with Pepper written on their stomachs. They're so tacky.

That's bothering me. The sheets of paper have got all the details of my trip to Canada. I'm flying first class, which is another world, a world we don't live in, Mum and me.

This business of me living with Mum, Dad living in Canada and him sending me stuff gets really complicated at times. I get home before Mum most days and, looking at the sheets of paper, knowing what is on them, what it will mean, makes me uncomfortable. Why don't I just tell her? Why can't I just come out with it? Why can't I just tell her that Dad's sent me tickets to go over to see him?

Why can't I do that? I don't know, all I know is that if I leave the sheets of paper amongst the pile of junk mail, then Mum knows that I'm not making a big deal out of it.

I was glad the house was empty, glad that I didn't have to say anything to Mum, well not yet. We get on alright most of the time, but whenever something from Dad arrives, there's this whole area of difficulty between us. Whatever he sends, we both know it's there and we both ignore it. We talk around it, over it, as if it was a bomb or something. After a while, Mum will ask, "What did your Dad send you?" Then I know it's OK to talk about it.

I took a can of *Coke* from the fridge. Mum writes notes for me, telling me things she wants me to do when I get home from school. One was stuck to the fridge door: *Peel potatoes and carrots. Lay table.* Usual stuff. Sometimes she'll write: *Wash a lettuce, prepare salad.* Then I know she'll be banging on about going on another diet. That's when she'll put the biscuits in the cupboard on top of the fridge, as if that'll make a difference. No diet today though, as she'd taken out four sausages from the freezer. They were lying in a bowl on the windowsill.

I picked up the sheets of paper. It was all there: the flight times, the boarding pass, stuff on weight allowances, everything I should know about my trip to Toronto. I don't know why I read it again, I knew what it said. I've seen it all before.

Maybe, by leaving the sheets of paper on the pile of mail, I was letting Mum know that I wasn't that bothered. It's not that big a deal. Flying to Canada to see my Dad. Been there, done that.

I drank the *Coke* and began to peel the potatoes. Mum would be home at around 6 o'clock. She wasn't on a late shift this week. It's just gone 5 o'clock. That's time enough for me to get out of this disgusting uniform. Lay the table first, what's that, five seconds? I'll have time to check my emails, to see if there's anything else from Dad.

There was a message from Dad. He wanted to know if I've received everything. Well, yes I have. It's all sitting on the kitchen table, but I don't want to tell him that yet. I'll wait until Mum gets home. Not sure why I am doing this, what difference does it make? Somehow, it just does.

I can hear the front door, Mum's early. I know the words that will come out of her mouth. She says the same thing nearly every day: "Christ, I'm knackered. My feet feel as if they've been boiled." My Mum works in a car rental office at the airport. She hates it, hates every moment of it, but she's forty-nine and says she'll never find another job. I don't know if that's true, but she says we live in an ageist society and once you reach fifty, you're on the scrap heap. She says she'll never tell anyone when she reaches fifty, but how will that work? I mean, there's PAYE, tax codes, personal pensions, all that stuff. How wouldn't they find out?

"Hi, Hannah, you upstairs?"

Yeah, I'm here, I'm always here.

"Yeah, just going through my schoolbag, checking my homework. I'll be down in a minute."

"Right, I'll put the potatoes on. Bangers and mash OK with you for tea?"

"Yeah, fine."

I can hear her rattling around in the kitchen, hear the sound of the tap running. She'll be coming up the stairs in a minute to get changed; she hates her uniform too. It's almost as bad as mine.

Here she comes, she rattles the handle on my door as she goes past. She does that most days. She lets me know she's home.

She didn't come in, she must have been standing outside my door. "That's it, diet on Monday. Button on my skirt popped off. Spent all day yanking it up."

I heard her bedroom door close. The house was silent again, Mum in her bedroom and me in mine.

Tea was OK, pretty much the same as always. Mum was going on about her job again. She doesn't want me to agree with her, she says she just wants me to listen: "...so when I realised the Renault had a full tank of petrol, I said he could have that one for the same price." She was quiet for a moment and then she cleared her throat. I knew something was coming. Dad used to say she was sharpening her voice.

"Hannah? That new bloke, Martin, well he's asked me out again. What d'you think?"

"Muuum! We've been through this like a zillion times. What's to think about? He's divorced, you're divorced, he's got a son, you've got a daughter, you both live in the same city. Why not?"

Mum twiddled with her fork, there was a piece of sausage left on it. If I know Mum, she'll be thinking about leaving it, that would make her feel virtuous. It doesn't matter that she's already eaten all the mashed potato.

Her head was bent over her plate and I could see fine, grey hairs peeping out amongst the dark brown.

"Wish I was your age again, everything is so easy with you. Just make a decision, do it, that's it, piece of cake." She still had her head down, obviously thinking about that last piece of sausage.

All of a sudden, I felt mean and I leant over to touch her arm. "Mum, it *is* that easy. Go out with this Martin. He seems like a nice enough bloke. If it doesn't work out, if he doesn't float your boat, then you don't have to go out with him again. There, sorted."

"But we work together, what about that?"

I watched as she put the piece of sausage in her mouth. "It still isn't a big deal. If it works out, you have a bit of bonking in the back seat of his car and, if it doesn't work out, you ignore each other. See, it's still sorted."

She chewed slowly and lifted her head to look at me. "Is everything that easy for you? That *sorted?*"

I shook my head, thinking of the sheets of paper. "No, but this really isn't a big deal for you either, Mum. Go on, go out with him, you could do with a night out."

She smiled, "Well, I'll think about it. I'd feel better about myself if I could lose a stone or two. OK, Hannah, you get yourself upstairs and make a start on your homework. I'll sort this lot out." She jerked her head towards the plates. Neither of us had mentioned the sheets of paper.

I heard the theme tune from Eastenders. I've looked at my emails again, but there are no more messages, just the one from Dad:

Hi Hannah, just checking to see if everything has arrived. Let me know – OK? We're all looking forward to seeing you. Love Dad. xxxx

Four kisses. So that would be one from Dad, one each from the twins, Josh and Cort and one from Patti, Dad's wife. That still sounds weird, Dad's wife. I've just noticed too that he's sent this from his office, not from his home. His office is amazing, a real skyscraper. Dad took me there once. I think it was the first time I went to Toronto. I must have been, what, eight years old? I'd never thought about the meaning of the word, skyscraper. I'd asked Dad, "Does this really scrape the sky?"

When he left home, when he left Mum and me, that was hard and the fact that he'd gone to work in Canada made it a lot worse. He came back two or three times a year, flying over just to see me.

We did the stuff that fathers do with their kids when they don't live at home any more. We did the cinema, the zoo, the trips to restaurants and he bought me some amazing presents.

At first, I didn't realise what it must have done to Mum: me coming back here, my hands full of the latest presents, top of the range phones, *Gap* sweatshirts and *Nike* trainers. She never said much when Dad brought me back. She just said, "Thank you, it looks as if Hannah has had a good time."

They hovered in the doorway as if Dad was an uncle we only saw once a year.

When Dad phoned to say he was getting married again, he said things like, "It was a pretty fast decision. That's the way Canadians do things. We just decided to go ahead and get married."

I can remember putting the phone down quickly. It had to be quick because I wanted to say to him, "But you're *not* Canadian, you're my Dad. You only live there, it doesn't make you a Canadian."

That wasn't the only quick thing the Canadians did either. Six months later, in another phone call, he said, "Guess what? Patti's had twins, boys. We're calling them Josh and Cort. What d'you think? You've got brothers now."

Dad organised the tickets that time too. I was nervous about seeing Dad with the boys. He'd emailed and phoned and everything, but I hadn't seen him since he'd become someone else's Dad as well as mine.

That was such a strange visit. Patti was quiet the whole time and the boys, well, they weren't. They yelled and yelled. They screamed, both of them, all the time I was there. When Josh was asleep, Cort yelled and when he stopped, Josh started up again. It was murder on the eardrums.

Dad and I went out a lot. We walked around, looking at the

buildings. Dad called that area *downtown*. We shopped at *Eatons*, we ate huge sandwiches and we sat for ages on the benches overlooking the harbour. Dad messed about, he pretended to be a lighthouse, holding an ice cream cone in his hand. He said it was the light.

Dad knew I wasn't comfortable in their home. They don't live in a house like Mum and I do. They live in a big flat, though Patti calls it an *apartment*. It's huge, bigger than our house. Every room is pale as if the sun has bleached all the colour out of everything. Patti says the wood is blond. She keeps the sun out all day by pulling down these huge blinds that are on every window, so you stumble around in some sort of twilight. Totally weird.

When I went last year, the boys were two years old and that's why I'd gone. For their birthday, Patti had dressed them in identical outfits: dungarees in a check pattern, she called it *plaid*. Their wispy hair was gelled back and they had dark blue, suede boots on. They'd stopped yelling though. In fact, they hardly said a word, and neither did Patti, at least, not to me. I thought that, maybe, she'd left the blinds up and the sun had bleached them all.

She said she had a headache when Dad suggested a trip to Jellystone Park. I know Dad only suggested it for the twins. Patti said she didn't think the twins should go either. Can't remember why. Dad didn't argue or try to change her mind.

In the end, Dad and I didn't go there either. We went to Ben and Jerry's instead. They're here too in the UK, but the one Dad and I went to was incredible. It was huge with buckets and buckets of incredible ice cream. We were sitting in one of the booths, licking away at one of these humungous ice creams when Dad said, right out of the blue, "Patti wants another baby. She'd like a daughter next time."

"Oh, right." I relied on my mouth to work, because my head

couldn't cope with that.

Dad was digging the spoon right to the bottom of the ice cream. "I don't want another baby, another daughter. I've got one already." He leant over and touched my arm.

"Anyway," he said, "three kids are enough, actually they're more than enough."

I knew that Dad had paid the mortgage on our house at home and Mum paid the rest of the bills, and when Dad wanted me to go to a private school, he paid all the fees for that too. But what I *didn't* know was what to say to him after what he'd just told me. This seemed to me to be private stuff, behind closed doors stuff.

Dad had pushed his ice cream away. "Three is enough," he said it again, but this time it sounded like he was saying it to Patti, only she wasn't there.

"Ready to go?" He half-rose from his seat.

"Dad?" I wanted to stay a bit longer, just a little while before we had to go back to the boys and Patti and, anyway, I hadn't finished my ice cream. He sat down again.

"Hannah?"

"Dad?"

We were falling over ourselves to be polite. Dad smiled, "You first."

Everything I'd ever wanted to say to him since he left, all the words bashed up against each other inside my head. It wasn't a couple of days of unspoken words, it was years of them.

He said my name again and then leant over the table, putting his head close to mine.

Then I thought of Mum. I thought about her sitting in the lounge at home, watching TV, drinking the one glass of wine she allowed herself each night.

"Do you ever think about Mum?" That wasn't what I wanted to ask.

Dad looked surprised, "Your Mum? Well, sometimes I do. Why do you ask? She's all right, isn't she?"

I nodded, "She's fine." I dug another spoonful of ice cream from my dish.

Dad watched me for a while, he must have been waiting for me to say something else.

I couldn't look at him. "Do you miss us, me and Mum?"

He didn't speak for a while and I kept on digging more and more ice cream out of the sundae dish.

"I miss the early years, Hannah. The years when you were small, before things went wrong. I get a reminder of those years now with Josh and Cort. The times I had with you when you were small are very precious to me."

I didn't want to hear about Josh and Cort. I pushed my ice cream away.

When we got back that day, I felt even more uncomfortable around Patti. She's a tiny woman, really thin. Her wrists are about the size of birds' legs and she's got long fingernails. She always shrieks if she touches anything that might break them. I'd been chewing my nails back then, they were really gross. I was thirteen and I'd discovered a shop selling second-hand Doc Martens, and I had been wearing my favourite pair: they were dark purple and I'd bought pink Lurex laces to go with them. Mum said I'd been a bit late with the Gothic look.

The whole time I was with them, Patti skirted around me like I had some sort of force field. She wore shoes with kitten heels and they went *clack clack* whenever she walked across their blond wooden floor. My DM's left scuff marks, she rubbed at them when she thought I wasn't looking. She didn't have a clue about how to talk to me. "How are things at school? What d'you want to do when you leave? Have you thought about university?" I mean, come on! I do want to go to university. Wonder what she'd say if I told her I liked the sound of the one in Toronto. I was as glad to go as she was to see me leave.

Dad's been over since. We went to see *Wicked*. I didn't have the heart to tell him we'd been before, twice. After the show, we went to a restaurant and I asked about the boys, about Patti.

"Fine, they're all fine. They send their love." He took out some photos from his wallet and handed them over to me. The twins' faces stared out from one photo, the parting in the hair of each of the boys was so straight, I wondered if it had been done with a ruler. As Dad put the photos back inside his wallet, something on the other side caught my eye.

"Wait, what's that?" I tugged at the corner of the photo I'd seen. It was one of me. I'd been about six, I think. It was a school photo: a tie with a huge, lopsided knot, a navy cardigan and a bright, white blouse. My face was covered in freckles and my hand was trying to cover the gap in my front teeth.

"I carry that one with me all the time."

"Have you got one of Mum?" The words felt hot in my mouth.

"Your Mum, well no, I haven't."

"Why did you leave us, Dad?" My mouth felt burnt as if I'd swallowed hot food.

"Oh, Hannah, not now."

"When then? I've never asked you before, not once." I could feel stupid tears and I kept blinking to get rid of them.

"Has your mother put you up to this? Has she been talking to you?"

"*No!* She hardly ever mentions you."

There was silence after that. We both stared over each other's shoulder, hoping no one in the restaurant would notice that we weren't talking. A waiter came over, asking if everything was alright.

"Yes, thank you." Dad's voice was clipped.

The waiter walked off and Dad sighed, "Look, I won't bore you, but sometimes things between two people don't work out." He stopped and looked at me. "Are you sure you really want to know?"

"Yes."

He sat back and I felt my scalp tingling.

"Your mother and I drifted apart." He gave a brief laugh. "That sounds like a cliché, doesn't it?"

Yeah it did.

"She hadn't done anything wrong and neither had I, but the marriage was dead in the water. My job was taking me all over the place, I was working longer and longer hours. I hardly ever got home and, when I did, there was nothing to talk about."

"There was *me*, didn't you talk about me?"

His voice was soft, "Of course we did. You held us together for a long time."

"What, like glue?" I couldn't help it.

He frowned, "You started this, you wanted to know."

There was another silence, this time we both looked at our hands. Dad tugged at his wedding ring. He and Patti wore matching bands. The noise in the restaurant flowed around us while we sat not saying a word. I wondered what we looked like to other people.

Dad waved at a waiter, "I'll get the bill, it's getting late."

So that was it: the reason my parents divorced, there was no reason.

In the car going home, Dad kept turning his head to look at me. I saw his fingers drumming on the steering wheel. "Hannah?"

"What?" I'd had enough talking.

"Do you remember me saying that Patti wanted another baby?"

His tone was light, almost teasing.

"Yeah, why?"

"She wants a daughter."

"Yeah, you told me that."

"Look, Hannah, help me out here."

"I don't know what you want me to say, Dad." I felt tired, I just wanted to go home.

Dad frowned, "She loves the boys, we both do, it's just that she says she'd like a daughter."

"What has this got to do with me?"

"I'd like her to get to know you properly, let her see what a great girl you are."

Really?

"Why? I'm not her daughter, I'm yours and Mum's."

"Yes, of course you are." He swallowed, "Look, Hannah, what I'm trying to say is that I'd like you to be friends with Patti, and a sister to the boys. Spend time with them. I'm away a lot, travelling all over the place and I'd like to think of you all getting along when I'm not there."

"Oh, Dad. I don't know." *Spend time with Patti? Me?*

"Please, Hannah. Do it for me. Look, I'll level with you." He stopped talking and glanced at me before speaking again. "Things are not great right now and I really could do with your help. Another child, well, that's not something I'd planned for." He didn't say much after that except to ask me if I'd at least think about what he'd said.

Eastenders theme tune had started again, the programme must have finished.

Sitting on the bed, trying to look over my school books, none of it made sense. My head was full of Mum, the tickets, Toronto, Dad. I knew what the latest ticket was for, it wasn't about going over there to see them all. I knew what Dad wanted. More glue, more keeping things together. Playing at happy families, me being the daughter.

I got up and walked over to my laptop and typed in Dad's email address. If I sent this message to his office, he'd be on his own when he read it.

I went downstairs and asked Mum where she'd put the button from her skirt.

"Why?" She was sitting in the armchair, her fingers laced around a glass of wine.

"Thought I'd sew it on for you, OK?"

"Guilty conscience or something?"

"Don't make it into a big deal, it's only a button."

Before I went upstairs to get the button, I poured Mum another glass of wine.

Treading Water

When Steve told her that he wanted to change his name, for a moment Faye thought about doing the same. It hadn't been the first time that she'd thought about it. *Faye!* What sort of a name is Faye? It's an insubstantial name, one that sounds as if it would float off, like the seeds from dandelions, the seeds she'd blown over her father's bean trench. He'd told her off for that, telling her how the dandelions would grow and clog up his runner beans.

She dragged her thoughts back to her husband. He'd come home from work, tie askew, hair standing on end, looking every one of his 58 years. "I want to be called Jake."

Faye had been in the middle of chopping carrots, her thoughts had been on her mother and the conversation she'd had with her that morning

"*What?* What are you talking about?" She half-turned, frowning at him. "You can't just change your name, it's a complicated process. And why would you *want* to do it?"

She added, "You don't *look* like a Jake!", even though she didn't know what a Jake would look like.

Steve sank onto a chair, "I'm sick of being me, of having a bog standard name, of being one of five Steves in work. It's ridiculous. Someone yells "Steve," and we all turn to see which one is being called."

Faye had to admit it had sounded funny when Steve told her how many men with the same name were working at the City

Hall. Yes, some of them were in different departments, but there did seem to be a small army of Steves.

Faye turned back to the carrots, "You can't change your name, it's a ridiculous idea."

She heard the sigh from her husband, "I am so fed up."

"Changing your name won't make that better." She'd heard him say the same thing many times.

She kept her back to her husband, hearing the way he breathed. She knew, without turning, that he'd be putting his head to one side, then the other in an attempt to relieve tension. She heard the *click* as his neck moved. Then she heard him walk away and his footsteps sounded heavy.

Faye sighed too. It had been a trying day.

When her mother phoned, Faye recognised boredom in her mother's voice. "If I don't do something soon, well, I don't know what I'll do."

"What are you talking about, Mum? Do what?"

"Oh, it's all right for you, Faye. You've got a husband and your work…"

At this point, her mother's voice trailed off.

Faye's job, or lack of it, was something neither woman wanted to talk about. Faye had worked as a librarian at the Central Library, a large, imposing building where she'd been happy for more than twenty years. And then cut backs meant her job had disappeared, just like that, gone. To stave off boredom and frustration, Faye had been volunteering at an Amnesty bookshop where, to her surprise, she'd come to love the shop and its customers, and the other assorted volunteers. Her mother, Jenny, thought that Faye was wasting her talents, "After all, you've got a degree in English." And as for Steve, he voiced his concerns about the fact that Faye wasn't earning money.

Faye had stopped defending her time at the book shop, telling

Steve that she was looking for work but, in truth, she wasn't and she tried to ignore her mother's comments.

"What would you like to do, Mum?"

"Go on a cruise and I want you to come with me."

Her mother's words bolted, as if escaping.

"A *cruise!* With *me?*

"Well, yes, and why not with you?"

Faye knew she'd groaned and hoped her mother hadn't heard. What was it about her life lately that everyone assumed she was drifting, and available at all times? OK, the kids had gone, both of them living away from home, but Faye had things to *do*, to be part of, or at least, she felt that way.

"Oh, Mum, I don't know. A cruise, they're expensive and…"

Her mother rushed in as if she'd been anticipating Faye's reaction. "I'll pay. You know I'll pay. It's not a problem for me."

Faye felt her mother's loneliness was like a blanket, smothering her.

"Where had you thought of going?" As soon as she'd spoken, she realised that her mother would think she was agreeing and Faye closed her eyes.

"Only the Mediterranean, there are some lovely ports: Athens, Barcelona, Santorini…"

Only the Mediterranean.

Last year, she and Steve had gone to France, a camping trip which Steve had said would be good for them, "We can prove we're not past it, love, that we don't need five star hotels to have a good time."

Five star hotels? Faye would have settled for a leaky shed after spending a fortnight in a tent. Steve had later mumbled something about "the idea sounded better than the real thing."

Really?

Somehow, and Faye wasn't sure how, but her mother thought

that it was done and dusted, that Faye was in favour of going on a cruise with her. Faye had used phrases like "in theory," and "don't know if the dates work," vague, non-committal phrases, but Jenny had grabbed them, like a dog leaping for a ball. "Great, that's great."

"No, Mum, I haven't said…", but Jenny was already talking about cabin sizes.

When she'd put the phone down, Faye thought it might be an idea not to tell Steve about her mother's phone call.

Sitting opposite Steve whilst they were eating their evening meal, Faye half-listened to his tales of rejected appeals, of angry emails from disgruntled planners, "…so now they're talking about getting rid of streets altogether."

"Mmm," agreed Faye, thinking it was easier to drop the occasional murmur into Steve's speeches. He didn't need her feedback, not really.

She glanced at him, looking at the way his Adams' apple moved when he spoke. It wasn't attractive; maybe it was best that men had them, although she was sure that women would have found a method of disguising them. She thought about how scarves would be draped around women's necks. Faye wondered about the way her thoughts were meandering. She thought about Steve's 'entanglements'. That's what he'd called them, making his affairs sound like something in a complicated knitting pattern. "I got tangled up," was something he'd said too. Faye remembered how he'd described what he'd done, as if he'd fallen over branches left out in the road, or tripped over a child's toy. They were 'accidents', as if he hadn't looked where he was going. He hadn't had the balls to say he'd had affairs. He'd tried to make them sound as if they were of no importance, mistakes for which he couldn't be blamed. Might have happened to anybody. She hadn't viewed them like that.

He'd admitted to two, both women he worked with at the City Hall. They came on to him apparently, finding him irresistible, a magnet for their neglected lust. "Didn't mean a thing," he'd told Faye.

She could never work out why he felt that would help, or even why *any* man would think that.

She'd listened to him, seeing the red-rimmed eyes, the graze of stubble on his chin. She'd known, of course she'd known, but had wanted him to tell her, working out how long it would take him to confess.

He'd begged for her forgiveness, telling her his job was driving him mad, he was up against all sorts of bureaucracy, of interminable meetings, of the sheer grinding monotony of his work.

"So, to alleviate the stress of your job, you decided to sleep with other women? Have I got that right?"

"*No!* That's not what I said, no, I didn't mean it to come out that way."

Not wanting to look at him, Faye left the room and moved her things into the spare bedroom. She'd slept there for weeks, trying to work out what she should do. Steve tried, she wasn't sure of the right word that fitted his behaviour as he tried to make amends and, in the end, she came up with *wheedled*. She thought it was apt and left the gifts he bought her on the table where he'd placed them. She took grim satisfaction from the look on his face when he understood that she hadn't touched them.

When the boys, Daniel and Matthew, said they wanted to come home for Mothering Sunday, Faye moved back into the marital bedroom. "Only because the boys will be home," she told Steve. "If it wasn't for them, I'd stay put."

She slept as far away from him as possible, knowing that if she turned in the night, there was a strong possibility she'd fall out of bed. Steve spoke about "second chances", of "working our way through this".

"It's not an obstacle course," she told him. "I don't know what I want to do yet."

Something stopped her from telling her mother, or her sons. Why was that?

When the boys arrived home, Faye knew that she was watching her family as if from a distance. The boys were their usual mixture of teasing, telling their father that he was losing his hair and showering Faye with flowers, and sitting down as she put meals in front of them and talking rugby with Steve whilst Faye was clearing up around the three of them. At some point over the weekend, both boys cornered Faye, asking if she was all right. "Seem a bit quiet, Mum."

Faye smiled and told her sons that she was fine, maybe a bit tired. They accepted that.

When Faye was 16, her father left home one morning, to go to the station, and catch the 7.45 into London. He hadn't caught the train, well, not that one. He'd gone to Margate where he lived with another woman. Faye only knew the woman's name was Angela when her father told her. From the day he'd left home, Faye's mother had always referred to Angela as "that other woman".

It had been arranged that Faye would see her father once a week until the time she left for university. She thought they were both glad of an excuse to stop the uncomfortable meetings. He'd drifted out of her life with only a birthday or Christmas card containing a cheque for £20 to remind her of his existence.

Her mother had been furious and Faye knew that her mother's anger was more to do with the fact that she'd been left, which she found humiliating. "Abandoned is what I am," she'd told Faye.

Faye wondered what that made her. Had *she* been abandoned too? She thought she probably had been. When Faye's grandparents died, leaving their daughter, Jenny, with a sizeable legacy, Jenny settled into the life of a lone woman, filling her days with lunches with the few women friends she had. "I've given up on men," she told Faye. Faye wasn't sure if her mother had ever been attracted to another man. If she had, she'd kept quiet about it.

As for Faye, she did wonder about having a revenge affair, but decided she couldn't face it. And anyway, she thought the men in the library were either gay or had been married for a long time and had, over the years, come to resemble their wives, or at least, that's what Faye thought whenever she met the wives at a Christmas party.

She thought there might have been an opportunity at the Amnesty book shop, but the volunteers were often younger than her, between jobs or early retired, and trying to do the "right" thing. She heard that a lot, doing the "right thing" or "giving something back." She didn't work there for those reasons, she simply loved being around books, the silence of them, the covers, the names of the authors, each book lined up in its allotted space.

Steve was still talking and it was when he said he felt as if he was just "treading water" that Faye made up her mind.

"Mum asked me to go on a cruise with her and I think I'll go." She busied herself, trying to secure a stray piece of potato, missing the shock on Steve's face.

"A cruise! When and what about the cost? You know we were thinking of replacing the dining table."

"Mum said she'd pay." She skewered the potato and chewed on it.

"Are you serious?"

Faye nodded, "Yes, I think so."

Steve looked at her, "You really want to go with your mother?"

Faye had never discussed Steve's infidelity with anyone, not that she had a lot of close friends, but the affairs had burrowed deep and she didn't want to bring them up to the surface. Steve had asked her once if she'd told Jenny, and Faye told him she hadn't, not wanting her mother to grab hold of the affairs, to align herself to Faye, needing to find a common denominator between mother and daughter.

Faye lifted her head and looked at her husband. "Yes, I do."

Steve had made remarks like "all right for some," and "hope you know what you're doing," at intervals in the weeks before Faye went on the cruise. She ignored him and knew that he was jealous of the fact that she would be on a luxurious holiday without him. Was it part of her needing to get revenge for what he'd done? Maybe.

Her mother had insisted on paying for them to be collected from their homes by car to be driven to Southampton. Steve had grumbled, "I'd have taken you. You only had to ask."

She looked at him, "I shouldn't have had to ask."

He stood at the doorway as Faye and her mother drove away. Faye lifted her hand in a limp wave and knew he'd be watching until the car turned the corner.

At the dockside, a trio was playing *Sailing* and Faye smiled, thinking of the musicians on the Titanic.

Her mother had been talking of "cabins" and Faye had assumed they'd have one each, but to her surprise, her mother had booked one for them both, a twin-bedded cabin admittedly with a balcony, so Faye stifled her misgivings and unpacked her suitcase. She saw the clothes her mother had brought: swirly patterned skirts, tops with glittering necks and an assortment of shoes, nearly all with heels and straps that Faye thought might have caused her mother difficulty in putting on, never mind wearing. By contrast, Faye's clothes were bland, cotton or linen in pale, unassuming colours. Her shoes were worn, comfortable to wear, she hadn't bought anything new for the cruise, not wanting to spend money she wasn't earning. Faye saw her mother's disapproving glance at her clothes. She smiled and closed the wardrobe door. "Shall we go on deck and explore?"

The days passed in a haze of sunshine and the smell of suntan cream. It didn't take long for a pattern to emerge: breakfast was taken at the same table overlooking the sea and waiters gently flirted with Jenny and Faye, and Faye watched her mother lap up the attention. Then, after breakfast, a discussion on whether or not to take the day's excursion, a trip from the ship to the port and, if taken, a flurry of questions about what time they'd be returning to the ship. Then there was dinner, a formal meal with waiters balancing silver trays and tiny portions of beautifully cooked fish.One day, Faye wanted to see Santorini and her mother decided it was too hot for her. Faye wandered around the tiny streets, feeling the sun on the back of her neck. She gazed at the sea, the bougainvillea tumbling from balconies, the sight of the blue roofs of the tiny houses that encircled the harbour. The heat didn't bother her, she sat in the shade and drank from a bottle of water. She liked being on her own too, without the pincer-like grip of her mother's fingers on Faye's arm. Her mother didn't need any support when she walked, she just liked holding on to her daughter.

When it was time to return to the ship, Faye found her mother sitting on the deck, a tray of tea nearby. "Oh, there you are," her mother said. "Did you have a nice time?"

Before she opened her mouth to reply, Jenny began a story that

Faye had heard many times of a holiday that the three of them had taken when Faye was a child on a beach in Cornwall. Although Faye had no memory of the trip, she knew that, because of her mother's endless retelling, her memory was of her mother's story.

Jenny called for tea and, as they waited for the fresh pot to arrive, Jenny spoke to Faye. Faye had the odd sensation that her mother's words were muffled. She looked around at the people sitting on the deck, she heard laughter, the murmur of voices, it *all* seemed muffled, almost as if they were under water.

Faye closed her eyes, feeling the sun on her face. She felt inconsequential, she was just another person on a ship full of guests, all paying a lot of money for the privilege.

Shadows danced across her closed eyelids.

She knew that her mother was lonely, using money to bolster her, reliving the past, blaming Faye's Dad for leaving her without ever understanding that she could have done something with her life. Faye was aware of her mother's voice rising and falling. She smiled, as it sounded like whale music.

Faye thought of Steve, forever complaining about his job, his life, his *name*, always looking for a reason for his unhappiness. That's what his affairs had been about, his inability to do something about the things that were making him miserable.

And what about me? Faye kept her eyes shut, enjoying the closed in sensation, feeling a sort of darkness.

She didn't want to be like her mother, lonely and bored: reliving old hurts, making them the reason for her unhappiness. She didn't want to be like Steve either, lacking courage to change, blaming others for his mistakes.

So where did that leave her, stuck in a marriage that drained her? Why was she still there? She'd stayed in the same bedroom as Steve, not out of a wish to repair their marriage, but because she couldn't think of anything else to do. What did that mean?

It meant she was just like her mother, just like Steve: unable or unwilling to do anything about her life. She'd gone on this cruise only because of something Steve had said, "treading water". That's what she was doing, treading water.

She sat up and opened her eyes as the waiter brought them a tray of fresh tea.

The cruise had become a catalyst. The cruise liner was a world cut off from most things, the minutiae of daily lives: lawns to cut, bins to put out, supermarket shopping. It's a privileged world, but not one in which she wanted to spend more time. A week was enough, giving her a breathing space. She didn't want to be Steve's wife any longer, she'd outgrown him. She'd tell Steve that she wanted a divorce. She did, she knew that now. Time to move on.

Her mother had poured a cup of tea and held it out to Faye, "I expect you'd like to get changed before dinner." Her eyes raked over Faye's cotton trousers and chain store T-shirt.

Taking the tea, Faye shook her head, "No, don't think I do."

"Are you sure, Faye? I could lend you a few things…"

Faye smiled at her mother, "No, thank you, Mum. I'm good, thank you."

Shaking her head, Jenny said, "Sometimes, Faye, I wonder where you get your stubbornness from. Don't think it's from me."

Sipping at her tea, Faye kept quiet. *It's from me.*

Living Over the Shop

Lil pushed her legs down, trying to reach the bottom of the bed with her toes. She stretched out her arms, flexed fingers touching the cotton sheet, like a pianist touching the keys of a favourite piano. The entire bed was hers, she had it all to herself. She loved the richness of that feeling. No greasy marks on the pillow, no wiry hairs left on sheets, no guttural snoring and no harsh, groping hands to disturb her sleep.

Lil's outstretched fingers touched the bag of mint imperials she kept underneath one of the pillows. She popped four of the hard, white sweets into her mouth and sucked contentedly as she listened to the noise of her sons unloading the latest delivery. After her nap, she'd go downstairs and take a look at what they'd brought home. Rolling over to her left side, Lil found her handkerchief; she held the soft fabric to her face and breathed in deeply. She had a set of the fine, Irish linen handkerchiefs in her bedside drawer, dipping one handkerchief each week in the bottle of gin she kept in her bedroom. Lil held the handkerchief firmly to her nose and closed her eyes. She slept.

Lil had been living over the shop for all of her life. Her father started the business, *Earnshaw's House Clearance – Good Prices Paid for Clean Items*, when Lil was born. Lil had no idea who her mother was. Ernest, her father, had been vaguely surprised that she'd shown any interest in knowing.

"I didn't know her all that long," he told her. "She seemed quite keen on me. Took her out a few times in the van," he coughed. "Plenty of room in the back, if you know what I mean. She scarpered though after you came along."

After the war, when men returned home and began settling down into married life, Ernest Earnshaw saw a way of making money for himself and his motherless daughter: second hand furniture. Initially, he scoured the papers reading the death notices, then he'd go off in his big Morris van, talking to the families of the deceased, buying up sideboards, dressing tables, old bedsteads and mattresses, anything from which he thought he could make money.

The shop, and living over it, became Ernest's life. Lil grew up with the ringing of the shop bell. She spent her early years in a big play-pen, peering up at customers as they browsed or haggled with Ernest over prices. When someone eventually made an offer on the play-pen, Ernest moved Lil into an old tea-chest. He sanded down the edges and put soft dolls and toys inside for her. Lil thought everything in the world was just outside the tea chest: she stood on tip-toes, her fingers gripping the edges, her serious eyes watching her father in the shop.

The shop bell summoned Ernest from his meals, or from working on his accounts or doing the football pools. The sound of the bell reached him in the outside toilet where he did the crossword puzzles from the *Daily Express* when the day was quiet.

Lil was almost eighteen when Ernest died. He'd had a heart attack brought on by the excitement when he opened an envelope from Littlewoods Pools.

Dear Mr. Earnshaw,

We have great pleasure in enclosing our cheque for....

Lil was certain her Dad never saw the amount he'd won... £50.

Lil read the letter after taking it gently from Ernest's fingers as he lay slumped over a walnut table he'd bought the week before.

Even in death, she thought that Ernest was thinking of the shop and its trade. He died on a Thursday and was the first burial on the following Monday, so Lil only lost one morning of trade. She'd inherited the shop and all of its contents, together with the £50 that her Dad had won. Lil was nervous about the money in the metal box which Ernest had kept under his bed. That was money for stock, so she thought she should keep it there, the way Ernest had done. She spent some of the Pools' money on a new gas cooker and cans of duck egg blue paint. A few weeks after Ernest's funeral, Lil painted the kitchen of the flat. On the morning of her eighteenth birthday, she walked into the best hairdressers in town and asked them to bleach her dark brown hair. She paid with the remainder of Ernest's winnings and left the salon with her hair glittering like newly minted sovereigns. With the leftover paint, Lil carefully stencilled the name of her business on Ernest's van: *Lillian Earnshaw: Emporium for Used Furniture.*

She was proud of the word, *emporium.* She liked the weight and the length of the word, she thought it gave the shop class, substance. She'd always loved reading and, on the days when Ernest had sent her to school, she practised her reading and spelling diligently. She didn't know anyone from the local girls' school. When she went into the classroom, she found that those she'd sat alongside on one occasion, had moved up to another class by the time she went again.

Boys were totally unknown to her. Whenever she passed a group of lads in the street, she kept her head down until she'd walked by. If they made any comment on her freckles or her overlong dresses and old fashioned shoes, she didn't acknowledge them or make any sign that she'd heard. Boys were like a foreign language she listened to, yet couldn't understand.

After Ernest's death, Lil realised that she'd need help to run her business properly. She had no family, she knew of no cousin or aunt to help. Apart from anything else, there was the problem of Wednesday afternoons.

For as long as she could remember, Ernest had closed the shop at one o'clock each Wednesday and settled Lil in the passenger seat of the van. The drumming of the engine was reassuringly loud in the empty expanse of the Morris as Ernest and Lil toured the surrounding towns and villages, looking for three-piece suites, old cookers and rolls of carpet. Lil always sat quietly, watching her Dad's hands on the steering wheel. She'd sneak a look at him, watching the way his lips pursed as he whistled, she looked at the stub of a pencil jammed above his left ear.

On the return trips, with the roar of the Morris engine cushioned by the amount of furniture stacked up in the back, they'd stop off before going home to buy fish and chips for their supper. Lil's memories of the greasy paper, the fish in batter, were inextricably linked with the smell of other people's furniture, piled up high in the back.

But now she was on her own and Lil didn't know how to drive.

Wednesday was still an early closing day and she'd always need new stock, so she arranged with the owner of a local driving school to take her out on Sunday afternoons. The driving school only had one car, a sleek, dark blue Ford Zephyr. It had a bench seat in the front, in cream, mock leather and a column gear change.

When Lil got in the car, she giggled as her toes dipped towards the pedals. "It's just like the time my Dad wanted me to learn how to play that big piano he bought. Couldn't reach those pedals either, so Dad had to sell the piano at a loss."

The instructor smiled at her, his eyes focusing on the sight of Lil's soft, rounded knees, encased in *American Tan* stockings as she wriggled on the slippery mock leather seat. He brought a cushion with him for their lessons, positioning it underneath Lil each time she got into the Zephyr.

Lil passed her driving test first time although, by then, it was a struggle to fit behind the steering wheel. Her first son, Terry, was born just before Christmas. Lil never could remember Terry's father's name. She had a feeling it was Gordon. "Well, a name like that anyway, you know, a posh name," she told Terry years later. He thought it probably had more to do with the gin she liked.

Lil took on a sixteen-year-old girl to help her in the shop. On her Wednesday afternoon buying trips, Lil strapped her infant son in the front seat of the Morris, just as Ernest had done with her.

Terry was barely a year old when Lil's second son, Davey, was born. There was still plenty of room in the old tea-chest for two toddlers. Lil peered over the top of the chest as she walked back and forth across the floor of the shop. "You playing together nicely? Good boys."

Lil thought Davey's Dad had been a driver for a local auction house. Sometimes, when a piece of furniture was proving difficult to sell, Lil rang the offices of two old, established auction houses, and their vans would come to pick up the furniture and then sell it for her. The drivers for both firms were about the same age and both had blue eyes.

So, as Davey was born with a shock of blond hair and pale blue eyes, Lil told him later, "See, it could have been either of them, doesn't matter which one, does it? They were both nice to me, buying me fish and chips when we went out. No harm done, is there?"

Put like that, Davey had to agree. No harm done.

Lil was determined that her boys did not miss out on their schooling as she had. On the day when Davey was old enough to join his brother at the local school, she walked them to the gates of the red-brick building. There was enough force in Lil's beaming smile to propel both boys into the schoolyard. As soon as Lil returned to the shop, she took the old tea-chest into her store-room. Her hands lingered on the edges of the chest, smoothed and sanded lovingly by Ernest all those years ago. Her eyes watered slightly as she saw the marks of tiny baby teeth in the soft varnish.

The boys flourished at school, Terry showed an aptitude for maths, and Davey, to her delight, brought home his stories for her to read.

"Look, Mum, I looked up the word *emporium*. Miss wanted to know where I'd seen it. She didn't believe me when I told her it was on our van."

Lil felt they were a proper family. The days were full, the shop was doing well. They didn't need interference from fathers, cluttering up their lives. They could cope.

When she was sick for the fourth morning in succession, Lil put it down to the pork pies she'd bought that weekend from the corner shop.

"God knows how old they were," she told the shopkeeper. "That's the last time I buy any from you, you should be reported."

It was only when she walked to the end of the road to wait for Terry and Davey as they came out of school, that Lil realised that neither of the boys had been ill and they'd all eaten the pies for supper.

"Oh, God, not again."

This time, Lil didn't have a clue who the father might be. She'd lay awake for hours at night, running her hands on the mound of her stomach. Her mind raced up and down different memories, like a car trapped in a one-way system.

Then, just after her third son was born, Lil remembered. She'd joined the local Small Business Association. For their first function, they held a dinner-dance, a 'Get to Know Your Fellow Traders

Dinner', it had been called. She hadn't remembered that night particularly well, because, instead of her usual gin, she'd been drinking rum. It was actually white rum and coke, the *in* drink and "all the rage", everyone at the dinner dance told her. She'd had a lot of rum and, that night, Lil got to know her fellow traders. One confided to Lil that he'd been lonely since his wife died and he was thinking of emigrating.

When she cradled her new-born son, Lil whispered to the baby, "You started life on the back seat of a car, where I could see the stars smiling down at me from the midnight sky."

The birth of her third son had stirred up Lil's memory, unlocking details of that night and, most of all, she remembered the car. The lonely bloke had a car, a convertible, a Standard Eight tourer. Lil had never been in an open-topped car before and she'd begged him to put the fabric roof down when they parked near the river, on the other side of town. She remembered looking up at the stars, listening to his plans for Australia.

"You could come with me, we could start all over again, a new life together," he'd whispered to her.

"*Me?* Leave the shop?" Lil laughed and hugged him again.

She'd no idea what his name had been, no matter how hard she tried, all she could remember was the car, but she named her new son James. She'd always had a thing for James Dean. Before long, James became Jim.

"Where's he going to sleep, Mum?" Terry asked. "He's not coming in with me and Davey. Davey's bad enough, he farts all night long and I can't breathe." Davey hit his brother and Lil walked away from their scrap.

She kept Jim with her in her room until he was three years old. She bought the entire contents of a house and, amidst the faded carpets and kidney shaped dressing table, were bunk beds. She found a single bed for Jim, and after that, Lil's three sons all slept in the one room and, for some time, Lil slept alone.

The boys grew, playing football in the tiny back garden and jostling for space in the bathroom. Lil could hear their voices each morning, arguing over whose turn it was to go first. Jim's voice was higher-pitched than those of his brothers. `Aw, come on, you've been in there for ages. Muuumm, tell them!'

Lil's Emporium flourished: second hand furniture became fashionable and the area surrounding Lil's terraced shop was a haven for bargain hunters and collectors of antiques. Lil bought the houses on either side of her shop and extended her premises. She'd had enough of listening to the boys' arguments about bathroom rights, so she extended the flat above the shop, adding an extra bathroom and a larger living room. The outside toilet, where Ernest used to sit with his crossword puzzles, was renovated and Lil used this light, airy building to store bigger pieces of furniture, giving prospective customers time and space to browse.

Never having met their fathers, and not knowing who they were, didn't appear to trouble the boys. Their world was Lil and the shop. As they left school, their teachers asked about their plans, about apprenticeships and, for Davey, university was mentioned.

"What for?" In turn, they asked the same questions of their teachers. "Our Mam needs us in the shop, plenty of work, always furniture to unload, vans to be driven."

As each son had left school, Lil bought him a van and had it painted in the same colours as Ernest's old Morris. Lil hired a signwriter to stencil in each boy's name on the driver's door. Her name was still on the sides of each van: *Lillian Earnshaw: Emporium for Used Furniture.*

Lil was content. Her world and that of her sons was contained inside her shop and the flat above. When she locked up the doors of the shop each Friday night, she'd walk to the pub at the end of the road where she sat for an hour, the ice in her glass of gin melting, as she smiled at the other regulars.

Sometimes, she'd bring a man home with her, someone new to the district who'd just popped in for a pint and company. Lil always urged her new-found friend to be quiet as he tiptoed upstairs to her flat. Lil had read somewhere that gin stopped babies being born so she kept two glasses and a bottle of Gordon's by her bedside. Just before the man clambered into bed with her, Lil insisted that they both drank large glasses of gin. No one questioned or argued with her logic. And Lil never became pregnant again.

"Not taking no more chances, my girl," she told her reflection each night as she skewered bright pink rollers into her hair. By now though, Lil was fifty-five and her hair was greying, her dark eyes were surrounded by deep lines and the contours of her body had settled into plump, comfortable curves.

As Lil aged, the boys took on more responsibility. When they drove their individual vans around the town, they saw houses displaying newly installed bow-fronted windows. The air around the narrow streets became thick with old, fine dust, as floorboards were sanded down and varnished. Front doors sported heavy brass numbers, and blowsy lace curtains were torn from windows and replaced with the straight lines of Venetian blinds.

"We need to get pine, mahogany, good solid stuff, Mum, that's what people need now. They don't want veneer or utility any longer, they want something they can strip down, find the original wood. They still want second-hand, but we must call it something else, *renovated* or *distressed*,"' Terry urged Lil one weekend.

"*Distressed*," Lil laughed at him. "What's that when it's at

111

home?"

The three of them tried to explain, falling over each other's words in their eagerness to get Lil involved in a new venture. "It's weathered, or treated in a special way. Making it look as if it's older than it really is."

Lil laughed, holding up a hand, "OK, OK, I get the message. I'd better take a look at this *distressed* furniture."

She'd laughed softly to herself in bed that night, thinking about their enthusiasm for the business. They were all adults, but they were just as keen as she'd been at their age. Lil pulled the pink eiderdown up to her chest and reached for the tumbler on the bedside table. She still kept a bottle of Gordon's gin by her bed, taking a few, small sips each night before settling down.

"Good stuff this," she told herself. "Must be, haven't had another baby, have I?"

But she hadn't made a trip to the pub for a long time. No stranger had climbed the stairs to Lil's bedroom for years.

The thumping downstairs grew louder forcing Lil awake.

"What? What's going on? I'm trying to have a nap. Terry, is that you? Stop making that racket. Have you bought that table? I'll be down in a minute."

Her eyes were open, it was still light, she could hear the sound of cars driving past. She fumbled around looking for her glasses, her hand knocking over the tumbler, spilling its contents. Lil watched, mesmerised as the liquid puddled out, slowly reaching the far corner of the bedside unit where it ran in a thin stream down on to the carpet.

"What a waste."

She eased herself up, *noise has stopped and now I'm wide awake. Wait till I get down those stairs, I'll sort those boys out.* Lil slowly swung her legs to the floor, her feet sliding into her worn slippers.

She pushed her feet in and stood up. Reaching for her dressing gown, Lil tugged the cord around her waist and shuffled her way towards her bedroom door. It had gone quiet, Lil couldn't hear a sound. She opened the door and peered out towards the landing. She thought she could see someone moving towards her.

"Terry? Is that you? I thought you were downstairs."

"It's me, Lil, it's Tracey," A soft hand reached out and touched Lil's cold fingers. "Come with me."

Lil felt a tug on her arm, "Who, who are *you*? Where are my boys?"

"They're here, the three of them, and they've brought their families to see you."

Lily looked into the face of the woman who was holding her arm. "Where? I want to see them."

"Of course you do, come with me. They're waiting to see you."

Tracey led Lil into the big day room. Sunshine streamed through wide picture windows, the tables dotted throughout the room gleamed with polish and two large vases of roses stood on either side of the fireplace. Sitting in a circle near the fireplace were the boys. There was Davey, Terry and Jim. Lil smiled, of course they were here with her. She waved at the children and at the three women who were sitting close by.

Tracey led her to a winged armchair and motioned for Lil to sit down.

Lil's three sons pulled their chairs closer to their mother and began talking, "Hello, Mum, you look good."

Lil tugged at her dressing gown. "Should have got changed, I'll need to get to work."

Terry leant over and held her hand. "No need for that, shop is closed today. It's Sunday, remember?"

Lil looked at him, she frowned. "Sunday?" Then, as if a cloud had moved, she remembered. Of course she remembered. She remembered it all. Everything. How big the shop had grown, how the boys had bought new premises, putting in managers into the new shops. A large fleet of blue vans, each one with *Earnshaw's Emporium* written on the sides travelling throughout the county, a web page with the company name, customers making bids on furniture. She remembered everything, of course she did, she remembered moving here, to the residential home.

She smiled at her family. She saw the glances between the grandchildren, the newest one, sitting on her mother's lap, staring at Lil with large, serious eyes. Lil cleared her throat, "Got no idea what time it is, is it too early for a drink? I could murder a gin and tonic."

She listened to the laughter as her family settled around her.

The Collection

Trevor began his collection of coat hangers with the one he saw hanging in Room 106 at the Grosvenor House Hotel, London. He was staying there as a guest of Halliwell Cars Ltd. Trevor worked for Halliwell's as a sales executive, and he'd been the company's leading salesman from 2010 through to 2015. His sales figures were held up for others to see, praised throughout the twelve showrooms that made up the Halliwell enterprise.

Trevor was a true salesman from the tip of his ox-blood loafers to the crown of his blow-dried hair. His suits were a mix of mohair and silk in pale grey or fine pinstripes. His skin gleamed like a well-polished apple. His aftershave was subtle, lingering in the air when he left his customers, taking their deposits and financial details with him to his office at the back of the car showroom. His sales figures were displayed in thick red lines, soaring over the green, blue and yellow lines of the other sales reps.

"Study Trevor, watch his every move, take a *degree* in Trevor!" That's what the Sales Director told the company's trainees. "You won't go far wrong if you follow Trevor."

In 2015, Halliwell's held their first conference at the Grosvenor House Hotel. It was planned as a special celebration: it was the company's fiftieth anniversary and, to mark the occasion, they were going to present the most successful salesman with a trophy. Naturally, the best sales figures were Trevor's. He'd walked steadily, gravely in his new black lace-up shoes, bought especially for the occasion, to the top table where the Chairman, J.D. Halliwell was sitting. A trophy, a miniature Morris 1000, the first car J.D. had sold, now condensed into a nine-inch gold replica, was on the table in front of J.D. Trevor was engraved on the front registration plate, *Mathews* engraved on the back.

"This is the *first* one, the first trophy. From now on, every year, whoever sells the most cars will receive one of these." J.D. held the gold car up in one hand, the other held Trevor's dry palm. Trevor was so close to the chairman, that he could see J.D.'s dentures slipping around in his mouth as the older man spoke to his employees.

Walking back to his table, acknowledging the applause with a restrained smile, Trevor handed the trophy over to his wife, Cheryl. She held it up to the light of the Grosvenor's heavy chandeliers.

"Look, Trev, they've spelt your name wrong…they've spelt Matthews with only one `t'. Well, that's not right, is it? You should tell someone."

Trevor told her not to mention it to anyone. "They'll think I don't appreciate it."

When the dinner dance was over and Cheryl and Trevor were putting their clothes away in the wardrobe, Trevor heard a *clunk*, a satisfyingly solid sound of the wooden hangers as he smoothed the lapels of his dinner jacket before hanging his suit up. Cheryl was ladling cream onto her face. She turned her head left to right as she wiped off her make-up with tissues. Her shoulders had deep red furrows where her bra had cut into her. The lines on her face tightened and then fell into folds as she turned her head back and forth, fastidiously cleansing her skin.

Trevor picked up the miniature Morris 1000 from the dressing table, his fingers tracing the engraved registration plates. His eyes stayed on the misspelling as he placed the trophy on the bedside unit, next to his wallet and velvet bow tie.

Cheryl's voice was muffled as she pulled her nightdress over her head.

"...do you think it will be?"

His eyes still on the Morris 1000, Trevor murmured, "What?"

"I like it here, in this hotel, it's really nice. Where d'you think it will be next year?"

Trevor yawned, "I heard someone say it'll be at the Grand, Brighton."

When he thought Cheryl was asleep, Trevor eased himself out of bed and took a gold-engraved coat hanger from the wardrobe and tucked it into his overnight bag.

The next conference was held at the Grand, but Trevor and Cheryl were not allocated one of the best rooms, no suite this time, no room overlooking the front. They had Room 390, their windows looked out over the tiny courtyard at the back of the hotel. An extractor fan whirred all night, pumping out smells of roast lamb, chicken curry and grilled bacon.

At the Dinner Dance, their table was close to the toilets. A parade of sales reps, both men and women, slapped Trevor on the back en route to the Gents and the Ladies throughout the evening.

"Hey, Trev, didn't see you over here, wondered where you were. How's it going? Haven't heard much from you lately, bet you didn't know our figures were up by twenty-five percent on last year."

As he felt each slap on his jacket, Trevor's mouth opened, he said the right words, his voice sounding as it always did, polished and confident.

"Yeah, heard you were doing well. Beginner's luck, mate, and you've got a showroom in a good position. You'd have to be deaf and dumb not to do well on that site. Still got a long way to go before you come anywhere near to beating me!"

Another slap on his back, a handshake, and then, as they walked away, Trevor's smile slipped.

*Our most successful salesman this year...*He watched Mark Jennings, twenty-three years old, straight from university with a degree in marketing, stride up to shake J.D.'s hand. Trevor narrowed his eyes, *kid's suit looks as if he's slept in it.* Mark's trousers fell in soft folds to black shoes. A gold earring twinkled from his left earlobe as he stood under the central chandelier.

All the chandeliers in the big ballroom tinkled as the applause thundered on. Trevor's hands were resting in his lap. It gave him satisfaction to know that he was the only one not clapping.

In their room that night, Cheryl began massaging skin tightening serum into the pouches of skin under her eyes. "God, I'm tired. It's no good, I can't be doing with late nights anymore."

Trevor held his suit in one hand and opened the wardrobe door. He reached inside for the wooden coat hanger. Its gold letters: *The Grand at Brighton* shimmered briefly before Trevor hung his suit up and quietly closed the door.

When Trevor and Cheryl checked out the next morning, the hanger was tucked into the side of Trevor's overnight bag. After they arrived home, he put it in the back of the built-in wardrobes in their bedroom. It nudged against the hanger from the Grosvenor House Hotel before swinging gently in the dark interior when Trevor closed the doors.

During the next twelve months, the chart that dominated the wall of the showroom sales office also dominated Trevor's thoughts.

His red line had stopped its upward trajectory and its bold loops, and now resembled old, sagging elastic. The yellow, green and blue lines were taut, thrusting forward leaving Trevor's red line behind. There'd been a time when it was rumoured that the sales charts would be consigned to the bin, but J.D. insisted on keeping them on a wall in each of his showrooms. Trevor thought the old man was behind in his thinking as it bothered him having to see the chart whenever he walked into the showroom. He felt it was mocking him.

There were six months to go before the next conference and rumour had it that it was to be held at the five-star Swallow Hotel in Bristol. The sales team bickered gently over their sales, jostling to be the first to greet a customer. Trevor waited until the junior sales team were at lunch, before he picked up his phone.

"Mr. Daniels? Philip? Hello, how are you? Trevor Matthews here, you remember Halliwell's? Thought about you the other day, how's the motor? 'Bout time you traded it, got a newer model. I can do a good deal for you right now. What mileage have you got on your car?"

His jaw ached with cheerfulness he didn't feel. Each time he put the phone down, he watched as the imprint of his hand faded from the phone's handset. Trevor watched the young sales team, watched as they moved, *glided* towards customers. It seemed he was never quite fast enough; new customers appeared the second he'd popped out for a sandwich and when customers did ask for him, it was usually on a Wednesday, Trevor's day off.

Cheryl grumbled about his payslips. "Barely covered the repayments for the conservatory this month. What's the matter with you? Lost your sparkle?"

One Saturday after a long, flat day in the showroom, Trevor

swung his car into the car park of the Moat House Hotel. He'd had a terrible day, only four customers all day and two of those were killing time whilst their wives were having their hair done in the salon opposite.

One drink, that's all. He made a silent promise to Cheryl.

He looked at the other drinkers. Solitary men munching on peanuts, a group of middle-aged women, the subdued lighting of the bar, dulling newly minted highlights in their hair. The women shrieked and pushed each other, quickly downing all the cocktails that the barman had made for them before they left, apparently on their way to a restaurant.

What the hell am I doing here? Trevor jumped off the stool and went in search of the toilets.

The corridors were deserted, the dusty blue carpet softened his footsteps. Right outside the Gents was a large chrome trolley. It was empty except for a heavy wooden coat hanger. *The Moathouse*, stencilled in dull gold lettering, glinted against the dark, redwood stain on the hanger.

Trevor's hand whipped out, grabbing the hanger and he jammed it under his jacket and then walked steadily outside to his car. He removed the hanger from his jacket and placed it on the passenger seat. Driving home, his left hand reached over, his fingers touching and smoothing the gold lettering.

"I'm home, what's for tea?" Trevor waited in the open doorway of his house until he heard Cheryl's voice above the sound of the radio in the kitchen.

"Bangers and mash, be on the table in five minutes."

Shutting the door quietly, Trevor ran upstairs to their bedroom. He could hear Cheryl singing along to *Tragedy*, her thin voice struggling to match the falsetto of the Bee Gees. He put his hand into the back of the wardrobe and pulled out the two hangers.

He left their bedroom and walked across the landing to the spare room. Teddy bears and a stuffed clown, adorned with bright orange hair, were sitting on a rocking chair near the window. A wooden cot was tucked in the corner. A quilt with its cover of *Winnie the Pooh* was folded neatly on the mattress of the cot. A mobile, with silver stars hanging from the light fitting, moved as Trevor walked across the room. He opened the door of the plain, white wardrobe. Pink and blue hangers holding knitted jackets, matinee coats, tiny sweaters, all covered in polythene, rocked as he hung the three wooden hangers at the back of the wardrobe.

After using the bathroom, he bounded downstairs and into the kitchen where Cheryl was serving up enormous clouds of mashed potato.

Cheryl worked Saturdays too. She was the head manicurist at the *Beauty Spot* salon. Her hands were on display each working day.

"S'no good clients coming in and wanting to pay good money for a manicure if I greet them with broken nails. Wouldn't be right, Trev, got to look after my hands."

She wore thick cotton gloves as she dolloped steaming hot mash onto their dinner plates. Although the gloves had bothered Trevor at first, he'd got used to the sight of them. Cheryl bought different colours and she liked red for the kitchen to match the tea towels. She wore blue for the times she used the vacuum cleaner and she wore thick, industrial gloves when cleaning out the bathroom.

"Good day?" she asked, pushing a plate over to Trevor.

He opened his mouth to answer, but Cheryl spoke again.

"Had to call the police again today. That massage parlour, blokes accosting clients again… one woman threatened to…"

Trevor swallowed his mashed potato. It tasted buttery and light. He knew Cheryl would happily prattle on for a while, and he wasn't expected to answer. *The Beauty Spot* salon occupied the ground floor of an ugly pre-war terraced block of shops and offices in the docklands. *Jade's Massage Parlour* was on the floor above the salon. The whole area was due for demolition.

"I mean, what with taxis dropping off some of the blokes and those tarts from upstairs, clients don't know which end is up no more…know what I mean, Trev?"

"Mmm." The mash was very good, hardly a lump in it

"Well, I said to the girls, do I look like one of those tarts?"

Trevor's eyes darted over to his wife. Dark roots nestled at the top of her scalp, the make-up laboriously applied that morning was flaking, patches of her skin glistening through the layers of foundation. His eyes fastened on her gloved hands as she cut through a sausage.

"Well, Trev, do I?"

"No, course you don't. Don't be daft."

He listened to Cheryl's snores, her hands, covered with her fine, cotton night gloves, were crossed over her breasts as she slept. Trevor eased himself out of bed and padded over to the spare room. He opened the wardrobe door and he moved the wooden hangers, enjoying the sound as the wood nudged together.

When he arrived at the showroom on Monday morning, the Sales Director was waiting. "You understand, Trev, nothing personal. It's just that this is regarded as our flagship showroom, the jewel in Halliwell's crown. Let young Mark run this for a while. He can cut his teeth while you take over at Prestbury."

The Prestbury branch had the smallest showroom in Halliwell's empire, tacked on the edge of a sprawling industrial site on the other side of the city. It was referred to as "the graveyard". He was being sent there to die, or at least his sales figures were. Trevor realised that as he listened in silence to the Sales Director thanking him. He was thanking him for his understanding, his loyalty. Trevor smiled as his hand was pumped up and down.

"When does the…?"

"No point in hanging about, give Mark your keys when he comes in. He'll want your car too. He's driving a hatchback at the minute, do a swap when he arrives."

Mark drove in an hour later, the tyres of the Golf squealing as he raced up to the car park. Trevor had cleared his desk, before picking up his gold Morris 1000 and he'd taken the *Barry Manilow* CDs from the navy blue saloon he'd been using. His car had air conditioning and electric windows. The hatchback had alloy wheels and twin exhaust pipes.

Trevor passed Mark as the young man sauntered into the showroom.

"All yours, mate," he said as he threw over the keys to car and office.

"Cheers, Trev, car's outside, you'll need petrol and the clutch is sticking."

Trevor walked over to the Golf and flung his CDs, trophy and jacket on the passenger seat. He filled the small car with petrol, noting with grim pleasure that it took exactly half the amount of petrol he normally used for his saloon. He waved briefly as he left the showroom.

A small hotel, an extension dwarfing the original building, caught his eye as he drove towards Prestbury. He pulled the Golf into an almost deserted car park. The reception area was empty, so Trevor looked around for a corridor leading to the bedrooms. He couldn't see any sign of a camera and he walked quietly along the stained carpet. He could tell anyone who stopped him that he'd merely called in for a cup of coffee and a visit to the Gents.

No-one stopped him and he paused outside Room 10. The door was ajar, the bed unmade and the wardrobe door hung open. He walked into the room, noting that the wardrobe was empty and Trevor reached into the back and his hand found a wooden hanger. The varnish felt smooth to his fingers. He lifted the hanger carefully and hid it under his jacket.

Prestbury was old, and had been Halliwell's original showroom. Faded marks on the pale, grey emulsion of the office walls were a reminder that J.D. had hung family portraits there before moving on to glossier premises. Trevor didn't put up a sales chart, he put a dried out spider plant into the dustbin and asked the office junior to clean the windows.

For the first few weeks of his occupancy, Trevor stared at the forecourt. Bunting that had been put up to mark the Queen's Golden Jubilee listlessly fluttered above the cars. Years of wind and rain had reduced the red, white and blue to shades of pale khaki.

Trevor stopped wearing his favourite cologne and hours of sitting at his desk caused his once neatly pressed trousers to become shiny, and the fine cloth sagged. The only customers who came through the glass doors were middle-aged family men looking for a cheap car for a son or daughter, or a *run-around for the wife*. The absence of a sales chart somehow made things worse, but Trevor didn't have the heart to do anything about it.

Trevor soon realised that he spent most of his working day watching the clocks on the wall of the showroom. J.D. believed it might impress customers if, as they walked through the doors of the showroom, they could see a battery of clocks on the opposite wall. The clocks showed the different times in New York, Hong Kong, Toronto, Mombasa and Delhi. J.D. had used it as a sales gimmick for years. He'd instructed all his sales team to take photos of their bemused customers standing under one of the clocks.

Later, when the new owner collected his car, he'd find amongst the service book and warrantee details, a framed photograph taken with a salesman and a caption which read: *Halliwell's Break All Time Barriers.*

Trevor no longer worried about his lack of success, he kept his eyes fixed on the hands of the UK clock, he was waiting until he could leave Prestbury and renew his search. He began keeping a record of where he'd found good quality hangers and where he'd been disturbed and had left with nothing. Sometimes he found unlocked rooms, and sometimes, like the first time, he found unattended trolleys where coat hangers just hung, unsupervised and unloved.

The city had many hotels: business hotels, large and small hotels and, daringly, Trevor even looked through the corridors of B&Bs. Some of those had uneven floors and crooked walls where the floorboards creaked as he walked through searching for new hangers. Trevor felt no fear as he walked down corridors. He was never stopped or questioned. He thought he *merged* with the small army of people he saw on his forays.

There were always people, mostly men, huddled around the bars of anonymous hotels or silently walking the corridors, a key in one hand, briefcase or overnight bag in the other. Trevor kept a soft holdall in his car and he carried this with him as he wandered through corridors. It served two purposes he thought: he looked as if he belonged in the hotel and, of course, on a successful trip, he could put hangers in there. They had to be wooden, the coat hangers *must* be wooden, gold lettering was a bonus, but he'd never take wire coat hangers. What was the point of that?

After each trip Trevor put the hangers in the white wardrobe, going in there when he knew that Cheryl was asleep. He quite often stayed in the room for a while, moving the hangers against each other so he could hear them *thud*. He had so many wooden hangers, the baby clothes were squashed together. He knew Cheryl never entered the spare room. She'd started buying baby clothes not long after they were married. She'd burst through the front door, her face wreathed in smiles and excitement, rarely bothering to take her coat off before showing Trevor the tiny garments she'd bought that day. He'd smile at her gently before asking, "What's the hurry, we've got plenty of time."

Cheryl stopped buying baby clothes when she reached her fortieth birthday. They'd never been able to afford specialist treatment and, over the years, that area of their lives gradually became submerged, buried between them. Trevor asked once if it might be better if he got rid of the baby clothes, the mobile and the cot.

"Why?" Cheryl's sandy lashes trembled with the weight of tears. "Not doing any harm up there, are they?"

"Course not, love. I just thought you'd prefer it if they were somewhere else."

"Leave them, Trev. I won't go in there again. I can't, there's no point, but I like to know that everything's there. I need to know that. Leave them, please." She never mentioned them again.

The invitation to the Swallow Hotel Conference was on the kitchen table when Trevor arrived home one night. Its thick, cream envelope lay on top of an envelope from the gas company and a reminder from BT. Cheryl never opened the mail, she rarely received letters solely addressed to her. She regarded bills and any official envelopes as Trevor's responsibility.

"When is it, love?" she asked as he read out the invitation.

"End of March, we've got a room at the Swallow."

"Need a new outfit for that and shoes." Cheryl lifted a casserole from the oven.

"Can't you wear something from your wardrobe? We're not exactly rolling in it these days. These are bills for the phone and gas. We've got to cut down."

"Oh, don't start. Always grumbling about money, that's all you do lately. Sell a few more cars, get your finger out, do some overtime or something."

Trevor watched in silence as Cheryl's hands, encased in thick red gloves, spooned chicken casserole onto their plates.

When they arrived at the Swallow, Cheryl was delighted by the grandeur of the hotel. She grabbed Trevor's arm in excitement and her shoes clacked on the marble floor as they walked over to the Reception. They were given keys to Room 205 and were shown the way by a silent maroon-uniformed porter. Cheryl kept her eyes fixed on the panel in the lift, watching the numbers change as the lift glided upwards. Trevor's eyes were focused on the large stainless steel trolley where the porter had placed their bags. Two wooden coat hangers bumped together as the lift rose.

The lights of the Banqueting Suite shone on the guests as applause shook the room. "Mark has smashed all previous records, he's set new heights in car sales…" Trevor heard the way some of the guests were banging the tables, whooping and calling Mark's name as the applause thundered on.

He stood, "Won't be long, love," he told Cheryl, and he left the room, shaking hands with some of the other salesmen and their wives, patting on backs and giving a friendly wave to the Sales Director as he walked towards the exit.

The maroon carpet along the corridors of the Swallow Hotel was thick and luxurious, the pile absorbing the sound of Trevor's footsteps as he walked. No one saw him as he moved silently, determinedly towards Room 205. Pushing the door open, traces of Cheryl's cologne still hung in the air, cans of hairspray and deodorant lay on the bed.

Trevor opened the wardrobe door. He'd pushed the coat hangers to the back, hiding them so that Cheryl wouldn't use them, smother them with her coat, skirt and blouse. He threw all the other hangers onto the floor. There were only two left. Their gold lettering twinkled at him. He stepped into the wardrobe and closed the door.

The Photographs

It was after your grandmother died, your Nanna, that I found the photographs. They'd been lying underneath a pile of books. The edges had curled, peering out from underneath the books. There were five black and white photos, the images were still clear. I remember the day they were taken. It had been late October, leaves were falling and the three of you were perched on the low branches of the trees we'd found.

I'd taken the three of you to the woods; we were going to have a treasure hunt and I'd dressed you warmly, putting on layers of clothing: hand-knitted jumpers, woolly socks. I wanted you to be warm, but I wanted you to look good too. I wanted you to look happy, well cared for. You were having your photographs taken.

You were anxious to do exactly what the photographer was asking of you. I'd explained that he was a *real* photographer, someone who was paid for taking photos, not like me, who took endless pictures of the three of you, charting your progress, then keeping the results muddled together in a cardboard box on a shelf in the dining room.

When your Dad left, he also left the box of photographs. I never understood that. Surely he'd need them. Without them, he wouldn't have been able to see your faces every day. He never saw them, not these photos. He wasn't with us when they were taken. Alun was with us. You knew him. He'd been to our house, he'd sat in our garden, pushing you in turns on the squeaking red swing, ignoring my pleas of "Not too high!"

He was your Dad's friend. They'd gone to school together and they used to sit drinking and swapping memories, boasting about exploits with blocked toilets and non-attendances. After your Dad left, Alun would stay long after you'd all gone to bed. He'd stay while I ploughed through the ironing, while I put your gym kits together, folding Brownie uniforms, searching for missing socks.

When he came to see us after your Dad left, you saw the large bunch of flowers he held and each of you took the giant tubes of *Smarties* he'd brought for you. At the time, it seemed to me that you recognised he still came to the house. You appeared to accept that, where once he was your Dad's friend, now he was mine.

It had been his idea to take photos of you. "Let me do it properly," that's what he said. "They're beautiful children. Let me do them justice."

You were all intrigued by the camera, the lens that moved around. You watched in silence as he set it up, your eyes following him as he walked between sun-dappled clearings, trying to get the best light. You were silent because you seemed to understand that these photos were serious, not the disorganised pictures I took of you.

Without being told, you grasped each other's hands. You stood in a line waiting for the usual command: *smile*. But he didn't ask you to smile; he asked you to sit on an old branch near the base of a tree. You glanced at each other, bemused looks on your faces. For a while, the *click* of the shutter was the only sound. You sat perfectly still as Alun moved around you.

Then he asked the three of you to walk towards the camera and, once more you held hands as you fanned out, walking towards him. I watched you, from the sidelines, wondering what you were thinking.

When, a few days later, Alun brought the photos to show us, I was struck by the fact that you'd been so still, your faces gazing back at me. You looked wonderful, the shine on your carefully brushed hair, the way you formed a unit of three sisters.

I showed the photos to everyone, "Look at my girls." I showed them to your Nanna and Poppa. I saw the tears in my mother's eyes as she looked at them. My boss teased me, was I sure these beautiful children were mine? Neighbours asked if Alun would take photos of their children, but he refused.

I know I meant to buy frames for the photographs. I'd thought of hanging them in the hall, where I could see them each time I entered or left the house. I didn't buy any frames and we moved from that house and the photos somehow got lost in the upheaval.

Alun and I struggled with a relationship. We hovered around the fact that I was a newly single woman. He came to the new house; we sat in the garden in the summer and in the winter months, he sat on the mismatched chairs in the living room. He watched as you all began tap classes, saw how you struggled with spelling tests and he was there when we celebrated your birthdays with home-made chocolate cake. I so wanted you to like him, for my sake.

He asked me out to dinner, to the theatre, but after a while he seemed unwilling to understand that I needed reliable babysitters and these were hard to find. "Ask the woman at the end of the road." Once he said he felt sure the three of you would be all right on your own. "They're sensible kids." Eventually I realised that he was merely an observer, a bystander in your lives. He stopped coming round.

I hadn't thought of those photos for years.

You were 10, 8 and 6 when the pictures were taken. Thirty years later, I can still see the gloss on your hair. I remember knitting the warm sweaters you wore, choosing different colours for each of you.

I remembered the sunlight filtering through the remaining leaves. I heard the sound of our footsteps crunching over the multi-coloured woodland carpet again. I still remember the sound of the camera as it clicked.

What I did not remember was the look on your faces. Why hadn't I seen it before?

The photographs are sombre, your eyes are questioning, your faces solemn, there is no laughter there. Your heads are close together, as if protecting each other.

I've no idea how these photographs came to be hidden amongst my mother's effects. She loved the three of you, always spoke of her pride in you. Over the years, she displayed your school photos, your graduation photos, the glorious wedding day photos. But these five were hidden.

I took the photos home, placing them on the passenger seat of my car and, as I left Cardiff, my eyes flickered across to look at them many times.

Once home, I put them on my desk, my hands shifting them around, for some reason trying to remember the order in which they were taken. Why did that matter? When the tears came, it was because I could see what I had done, what my mother had seen and I had missed.

Now, I can see that the expressions on your faces were haunted, you were confused and frightened. You held each other's hands for support and comfort, the comfort you should have got from me.

It had only been a short while since your Dad left, a matter of months. I'd tried hard to soften the blow, to tell you that I would do everything to make sure your lives were not disrupted. Your Dad would still see you, he'd still love you.

I'd always known that one of the reasons Alun came to see your Dad was me. He'd made that clear a few years earlier. Part of me felt flattered. I'd be lying if I said anything else. And then, there were the lies I told. I told your Dad various stories: seeing an old friend, catching up with girls from school, going out with work colleagues. I told those lies smoothly to him. But I also told those lies to the three of you. I told you, my daughters, that "Mummy was seeing a friend from school." That always tore at me, still does.

"Who's your friend, do we know her?" This was asked by my daughters who filled the house with their friends. I said you didn't know her, we'd sat together in the classroom. You liked that, you laughed at the thought of your Mum wearing a school uniform, sitting behind a desk.

My marriage was dull, static and I'd been relieved when your Dad finally left. I thought I'd be a good single parent. I thought I'd cope well. I thought you'd accept the fact that I'd met someone else. I got it so wrong.

I let you down. That's the simple truth. It's in these photographs, your complete bewilderment, your uneasiness at the situation you found yourselves in.

Now I know why my Mum didn't display these photos, why she cried when she saw them for the first time. She could see what I could not.

I'm so sorry.

Also published by Watermark Press

Carole Hailey
The Book of Jem

In the aftermath of catastrophic religious wars, God has been banned.

As snow begins to fall, a young woman – Jem – arrives in Underhill.
The isolated community offers her shelter, unwittingly unleashing events that
threaten their very existence.

Jem announces that she has been sent to Underhill by God to prepare the
villagers to fulfil a devastating purpose. Some believe she is a prophet and defy
the law to join her God's Threads religion. Others are certain she is lying.

With their fragile community beginning to fracture, Eileen, the first and most
devoted of the believers, decides to record the birth of this new religion in her
own Book of Jem.

As God's Threads gather for the apocalypse, the words Eileen has written will
determine the fate of Underhill and, ultimately, of Jem herself. But can Eileen be
trusted to tell the truth? And how can anyone know what to believe?

'Bold storytelling, with the satirical force of Naomi Alderman's
***The Power* but its own claustrophobic sense of place.'**
FRANCIS SPUFFORD, author of *Golden Hill*

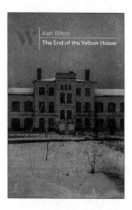

Alan Bilton
The End of the Yellow House

Central Russia, the black earth forest, near Voronezh, 1919. As the civil war rages, White forces, accompanied by feared Cossack divisions, advance ever closer to Moscow. In the chaos, the Yellow House, a sanatorium at Bezumiye, becomes cut off, the superintendent found murdered, a strange black box atop his head.

As the distinction between doctors and 'guests' frays, the murder sets in motion a nightmarish series of events involving mysterious experiments, the secret police, the Tsar's double, prophetic dreams, giant corpses, possessed cats, sorcery, and the overwhelming madness of war. Into this dangerously combustible mix, a ragged and eccentric police officer arrives, calling himself Inspector Tutyshkin and claiming he has travelled to the house to investigate the superintendent's suspicious demise.

But in this strange game of madness, doubles and disguises, are any of the players truly who they seem?

'A bold and confident novel that throws us into the deep end of post-revolutionary Russian life with fervour and wit. There are knowing nods to Gogol and Bulgakov but the voice is entirely original, with a gem of a phrase on every page.'
MARK BLAYNEY

'A brutal, but often witty and tender tale, *The End of the Yellow House* is a twistedly brilliant emotional rollercoaster.'
DAVID TOWSEY